QUAD

QUAD

C. G. WATSON

Quad

RAZORBILL

Published by the Penguin Group
Penguin Young Readers Group
345 Hudson Street, New York, New York 10014, U.S.A.
Penguin Group (USA) Inc., 375 Hudson Street, New York, New York 10014, U.S.A.
Penguin Group (Canada), 90 Eglinton Avenue East, Suite 700, Toronto, Ontario,
Canada M4P 2Y3 (a division of Pearson Penguin Canada Inc.)
Penguin Books Ltd, 80 Strand, London WC2R 0RL, England
Penguin Ireland, 25 St Stephen's Green, Dublin 2, Ireland (a division of Penguin
Books Ltd)
Penguin Group (Australia), 250 Camberwell Road, Camberwell, Victoria 3124,
Australia (a division of Pearson Australia Group Pty Ltd)
Penguin Books India Pvt Ltd, 11 Community Centre, Panchsheel Park, New Delhi –
110 017, India
Penguin Group (NZ), Cnr Airborne and Rosedale Roads, Albany, Auckland 1310,
New Zealand (a division of Pearson New Zealand Ltd)
Penguin Books (South Africa) (Pty) Ltd, 24 Sturdee Avenue, Rosebank, Johannesburg
2196, South Africa

Penguin Books Ltd, Registered Offices: 80 Strand, London WC2R 0RL, England

10 9 8 7 6 5 4 3 2 1

Library of Congress Cataloging-in-Publication Data is available

Printed in the United States of America

For Tom, Joel, and Rachel
that's my nice thing . . .

QUAD

THERE WAS A PEPSI machine on the west side of the student store. Ranger Ng thought about walking to the one at the gym instead, just to avoid a group of jocks leaning up against this one. But he needed a Mountain Dew bad. Before his head exploded. So he sucked it up and went over.

A stack of *Metros*—the underground newspaper that mysteriously circulated campus every couple of months—fluttered in the breeze, held in place under a hefty rock. Ranger shook his head. The *Metro* had first appeared on campus last year, quickly replacing the real school newspaper as a credible, if unofficial, news source.

Everyone read it. Even the teachers and administrators. They said it was trash, that they put no stock

1

in it, but it was obvious they'd come to rely on it to help "keep their ear to the ground."

In other words, to find out what was *really* going on in the hallowed halls of Muir High.

Ranger remembered last year's final issue: There was an article about a prank the seniors were planning, something about locking the freshmen in the gym and opening fire on them with paintball guns. Administration read the article and immediately rounded up those seniors who were identified by name. Chains and padlocks were found in one senior's car, and paintball rifles were found in the truck bed of another.

Those kids were banned from walking at graduation, while the rest of the senior class fumed, wondering who snitched on them. It was a pretty big deal.

Since the *Metro* had achieved such notoriety, everyone thought the paper's creator would reveal himself at the end of the year to soak up his fifteen minutes of fame. Rumor even had it that the teachers were placing bets on which of the AP-track Harvard-bound brainiacs it would be. But no one came forward, and just this fall, as people were beginning to forget about the *Metro* altogether, a new issue popped up.

Ranger had no doubt why this stack was still here: They were secured under a pretty big rock, and most of the lazy-ass students at Muir High weren't willing to work that hard for anything—not even a juicy bit of gossip.

Ranger pulled a fistful of coins out of his pocket. Two quarters clinked their way down the soda machine's gullet, then three, then four. As the fifth quarter was swallowed whole, Ranger heard a series of slow pops. Five in a row, the same number of quarters he'd just fed into the soda machine.

"Hey, Chink," Brad Calvert called over to him. "I hear fireworks. Is it Chinese New Year?"

"I wouldn't know, juicer," he muttered, his eyes fixed on the tray at the bottom of the machine. "I'm a gook, not a chink."

The Mountain Dew dropped into the tray with a heavy *thud*. Ranger bent to retrieve it.

"Not so fast, Lone Ranger." One of the other jocks stepped up, clapped a heavy hand onto Ranger's shoulder. "Where's your buddy Tonto?"

Calvert laughed so hard, he snorted Pepsi out of his nose. The rest of the steroid posse joined him.

But as their laughter surrounded Ranger, he realized he didn't actually know where his best friend was.

For Christ's sake, where is that crazy-ass Rufus hiding, anyway?

Pop!

There was the noise again—this time louder.

Ranger turned toward the quad, and the sound revealed itself for what it was. He watched people stop, listen, then begin to run. The truth slid down his back in rivulets, dripping onto the blistering concrete, one quivering drop of sweat at a time.

"Jesus Christ," he whispered. Then louder, "Jesus Christ, get inside!"

"Why?" Calvert asked, his words oozing with hate. "You freaks got some plan to corner us in there? You gonna use your kung fu on me, Chink?"

Pop!

"*Get inside!*" Ranger screamed this time, shoving Calvert and his buddies through the door with a strength he never knew he possessed.

"Dude, what the—"

"Get inside!" Ranger yelled, waving his arms as people passed by. "Get inside! Get inside!"

Pop!

Pop!

Pop!

Adrenaline shot through Ranger's body, coming out of his mouth in a blast of credibility. A flurry of students dashed past him into the student store. He began wondering how many could fit inside the small brick building. He looked around frantically until his eyes landed on a small sign over the door: Capacity—30.

Yeah, sure, he thought.

Cries of panic rang out from behind him, followed by another loud POP!

Ranger turned, saw the wave of fearful expressions.

Who would do this? he wondered. *Who would want to shoot up the quad?*

FREAKS

STONE LAUNCHED A FOOTBALL at the brick wall, two inches from where Ranger Ng and Rufus Dockins sat against it.

Rufus flinched—his first mistake. He silently cursed himself for it.

"Hey, you," Stone barked. "I need to use your gym locker for a while."

Rufus looked up from the book he was reading—tried to get his eyes to focus. "What?"

"*I need. To use. Your locker,*" Stone repeated, slow and close. He nosed right up to Rufus, threatening the most perfect triad of hair horns Rufus had ever mastered.

It took almost a full can of Aqua Net to get his hair fully erect that morning. If Stone ruined it, Rufus swore . . .

"I need it," Stone continued. "And you don't have anything in it, right?"

"Maybe I do, maybe I don't," Rufus argued. "That's not the point."

"Really? What *is* the point?" Stone mimicked Rufus's low-pitched delivery.

Rufus paused—squirmed under the heat of Stone's gaze. He glanced over at Ranger, who shot him a look of warning.

Rufus knew he shouldn't make too much of Stone's demands. There was no point in trying to fight, but sometimes—sometimes Rufus just couldn't help screwing with the jocks. It was too easy.

"The *point* is," he went on, "I don't want your sweaty nut bag touching my crap."

"My *nut bag*?" Stone's eyebrows arched. "You mean, my jockstrap, freak? You don't want my jockstrap touching your crap?" He shrugged and looked around. "What crap? You don't dress down for PE. So obviously you don't have any clothes in there. What're you trying to hide? Drugs?"

Rufus sneered. "Yeah, like I'm gonna tell you where my stash is. What the hell's wrong with your locker, Stoner?"

Stone averted his eyes before he grumbled, "It's full."

"Right." Rufus snorted. "Full of skeletons."

Stone growled, apparently out of patience. He slammed his fist against the wall. "Look, freak. I'm putting my crap in your locker, like it or not. And since you never open the damn thing, I expect you to stay out of it until I say you can go back in. Got it?"

"Whatever." Rufus shrugged, opening the thick sci-fi western he was reading.

Stone whipped the book out of his hands, losing Rufus's place. "Yeah," he grunted. "*Whatever.*"

He flung the book over his shoulder. Rufus watched in disgust as it landed in a nearby trash can.

Stone turned and ambled down the hallway, laughing. The rest of the steroid posse followed close behind him.

"Prick," Rufus muttered when they were a safe distance away.

"Dude," Ranger said, glancing briefly over his shoulder at the trash can. "Sorry about your book, man. That sucks."

Rufus shrugged again. It didn't matter. Not really. Because Stone had played right into his hands.

Stone didn't know it, of course, but Rufus had a plan. And he was going to have the last laugh in the end.

FREAKS

THE WHOLE LOCKER THING shouldn't have mattered. Because, in a way, Stone was right—Rufus hardly ever dressed for PE anymore.

But when the head juicer—Mr. Captain-of-the-football-team himself—demanded the use of Rufus's locker, Rufus couldn't exactly give it up without a fight.

That would have seemed too obvious.

Might even have spooked Stone away.

And then Rufus wouldn't have the sweet opportunity that lay before him.

It was one of those spring days that had started out winter and turned summer by lunch. Ranger asked if he could use Rufus's PE locker to stow his trench coat. With a sly smile, Rufus agreed. After all, they had waited long enough.

Ranger had long since relinquished the locker he was supposed to share with some freshman and now, as he dialed Rufus's combination, he told Rufus he wished he still had it.

"So why don't you go back and take it?" Rufus asked. "Hell, you're entitled, dude. Right?"

Ranger shrugged. "Nah, it's chill."

Rufus shook his head. No wonder Stone and the rest of the juicers always thought they could get over. He and Ranger couldn't even muster the energy to stand up to a puny little freshman.

Ranger pried open the gym locker's warped metal door. A chip of red paint shaped like Marilyn Manson fell onto the concrete floor at his feet.

Rufus waited. Yeah, Stone thought he could get over, but that was all about to change.

Ranger peered into the locker. Bolted back. "Whoa!" He nearly gagged. "What the hell, man!"

"What?" Rufus asked, still standing in the doorway.

"Smells like teen spirit, dude." Ranger's face wrinkled. "Like armpit and weed."

The armpit part made sense to Rufus—after all, it was a PE locker. But it was the other part—the second part—that was far more interesting.

"One of those juicers put his rags in my locker," Rufus reminded his friend. "But I don't think he was worried about stashing his jock. He was looking for a place to stash his *stash*."

"Whoa." Ranger frowned, moved closer to his friend. "What do you mean?"

Rufus nodded toward the locker. "You're the one with the nose. Check it out, dude." He leaned against the wall as Ranger dug around in the heap of fermenting gym clothes. He had a sixth sense that made him a bit of a celebrity in their circle: the guy could ferret out weed from two counties over.

It was poetic irony, they'd decided, when the school administration hired a drug-sniffing dog for random searches. The truth was, they could have just asked Ranger.

"Hey, must be your birthday." Ranger smiled as he pulled out the fat plastic bag hidden inside. A wide grin split through his pocked, uneven face.

Rufus paused, regarded the stuffed packet. "Got a light?" he asked.

"Yeah, *right*." Ranger frowned. "You know the fastest way to piss off a jock?"

"Yup. Steal their stash." Rufus nodded.

They stared at each other. Ranger's obsidian eyes flashed behind the black-rimmed glasses he wore just for show. He picked at a zit on his chin, contemplating the situation.

Rufus looked down at his checkered Vans and continued to wait. After ten years of friendship, he could tell exactly what Ranger was thinking: even though he was halfway tempted to steal the weed, he was terrified the steroid posse would come beat the crap out of them if they did.

Ranger tapped his foot on the linoleum tile double time, struggling to figure out his next move.

The sound annoyed the hell out of Rufus.

"Rally tomorrow, dude," he urged. "Perfect timing." He glanced at himself in the mirror at the end of the row. His pasty skin looked paler than normal. Sometimes Ranger called him a vampire, accusing him of fearing the naked light of day. Sometimes Ranger told Rufus he was the whitest white boy he knew.

"Christ, man! What if we get caught?" Ranger asked, breaking the silence. "The drug dogs haven't even been in here this month."

Rufus grinned. "All the more reason to get rid of it."

Ranger blew out a breath, raked a hand through his chin-length hair. "The steroid posse will kill us, you know. They'll turn into a pack of wild dogs and kill us till we're dead. I mean, it ain't like taking candy from a baby." He paused. "How long has it been in here? Like a week?"

Rufus contemplated. "At least. That dumbass probably doesn't even remember it's here."

Ranger's face twisted with doubt. "Bet me."

"So what if he *does* remember," Rufus pushed. "I'll just say my locker got broken into. I mean, dude . . . free weed. It's like finding a bag of money in the alley behind the bank." He blinked, shifted his weight to counter Ranger's lingering skepticism.

"No poor kid is gonna go without shoes if we take this," he pressed. "We know whose stuff it is, and we hate their guts."

Rufus could see his triceratops horns in the reflection off Ranger's glasses. They looked hella good.

As if he could read Rufus's mind, the same way he'd been able to since they'd met in second grade, Ranger agreed. "Your hair looks freakin' cool, dude."

Rufus sighed. "So?" he asked, ticking his gaze toward the plastic bag.

Ranger groaned. "Fine. Grab it and let's just get out of here."

JOCKS

KEN DAVIS WATCHED AS Stone pulled on his workout clothes, just as the last bell of the day was ringing.

"Is your ass on fire?" Ken smiled out of the corner of his mouth. "What's the rush?"

"It's three o'clock, dipshit," Stone said. "Just enough time for a special smoothie before weight training." He winked at Brad Calvert.

"Make mine a double," Calvert said, standing naked in front of his open locker. "I've been on academic probation all winter—I think I've gotten soft from not playing."

"Sure looks that way." Stone snorted, nodding in the direction of Calvert's crotch.

The guys in the locker room busted up. *Good one.*

Stone shook a plastic canister at Ken from inside his locker. "Dude. Want some?"

Ken held up a hand. "Pass."

"You sure?" Stone shook the container harder. "You might finally move up to first string next year."

Ken could feel his cheeks blazing. Stone had been using since JV football. One by one, most of the guys had joined him. But Ken did not want to get on *that* bandwagon.

Still, he knew what to expect if he made too big a deal out of it.

"I can't take that shit," Ken lied. "It'll kill me if I mix it with my meds."

Stone shrugged, replaced the canister inside his locker. "Your funeral. I hear those Lincoln guys are gonna be massive next year."

"Hey, Stone," Calvert called over his shoulder as he tugged on his gym shorts. "If that shit's so good, why don't you slip some of it to your old man?"

Most of the team cracked up. Ken pretended to laugh along, even though the joke wasn't very funny. He knew what was going on over at Stone's house. So did all the others—not that it seemed to matter.

Stone fixed his eyes on the bottle of water he was holding as he carefully tapped creatine powder into the narrow neck. "Right," he mumbled. "A little of this and maybe the old man will grow some balls for a change."

Ken narrowed his eyes as the other players continued to laugh. Stone had changed the moment his mom moved out. He'd lost some of his focus, was more on edge, even his sense of humor had become . . . darker.

And now he was wisecracking about his dad? Something about it seemed off. But Calvert kept right on. "Can't you just see Stone's scrawny old man?" he howled. "All pumped up, draggin' his mom back to the cave by her hair?"

Stone smiled. It wasn't a whole smile, really. It was . . . hollow. He shook his water bottle to get the creatine powder mixed in evenly. "Funny," he said. He started chugging.

"But I mean, your dad's such a wimp, your mom would probably beat him over the head with his own club first!"

Stone wiped his mouth on the sleeve of his shirt—flashed Calvert a warning glance.

"Dude," Calvert continued. "Remember that time you said that your mom got so mad she—"

Stone spun around, grabbed his locker door, and slammed it shut, using way more force than necessary.

The sound of the metal door echoed through the room—made Ken and a few of the other guys wince.

Everything else fell silent.

Stone's eyes drilled into Calvert's.

Then he grabbed a towel, threw it over his shoulder, and headed for the weight room.

The rest of the guys stared at each other, slack-jawed. Finally Ted Hooks let out a nervous chuckle.

"Well, fuck me," he said, closing his locker door and spinning the combination a couple of times.

"There's a short goddamn fuse," Calvert agreed.

Exactly, Ken thought. *A short fuse—on a time bomb ready to explode.*

He closed his eyes. For a second, he could almost hear it.

Tick tick tick tick tick . . .

PREPS

BRITTANY SMITH FELT A sharp pinch on her right butt cheek as she walked into history.

"Ow!" she yelped, spinning around. "What the hell?"

Stone grinned. "It's St. Patrick's Day."

"So?!"

"You're not wearing green," he informed her.

"Yes, I am. God!"

"Where?"

"Right here!" She pointed out a thin green pinstripe wedged between wide bands of maroon and gold on her T-shirt.

Stone scoffed. "That's totally minuscule!"

"It's *green*, Stone. That's all that matters. So now I get to pinch you back."

Stoned backed away. "I don't think so."

"Oh, *I* think so." Brittany beamed. "And I get to decide where." She lurched forward, bumping into Sage Wood's desk. Sage was French-braiding her pigtails and lost a twist when she took the hit.

"Oh my God!" Nicole McClintock, Brittany's best friend, dashed to the front row and parked herself on top of Sage's desk. It wasn't that Nicole and Sage were friends—hardly—but the best view of the Brittany-and-Stone show was definitely from the front of the class.

"Get him, Brit!" Nicole cheered.

Brittany reached out and grabbed one of Stone's nipples, twisting as hard as she could. Stone's eyes crisscrossed in pain.

Nicole laughed then, so hard that it made her stomach hurt. She clutched herself around the middle, then fell off the desk, sending her miniskirt flying up around her waist.

From her position on the floor, she could see everyone turn to take in her St. Patrick's Day thong, conspicuously exposed in the mishap.

"Omigod!" she yelped, rolling to her side and smoothing her skirt underneath her.

The class was a sea of hysteria by the time Mr. Morgan walked in, holding his ever-present cup of coffee. Brittany slammed right into it as she attempted to dodge Stone's counterattack. A dark brown wave rose up out of the stained mug—hung suspended in midair—before spraying like surf all over Morgan's pale blue shirt. And because he chose that day to wear a green pocket kerchief instead of a tie, Nicole thought that Mr. Morgan suddenly looked like the pull-down map that he used for his lessons.

A hush settled over the classroom as Nicole watched Morgan's face turn from its customary gray to deep, dark red. His mouth opened, and for a few terrifying seconds, nothing came out.

Then, two strangled words from between his clenched teeth: "Pop! Quiz!"

Nicole leapt up from the floor. Students hurried to their desks, and within seconds there was a renewed sense of order. An uneasy silence crept into every corner of the classroom.

And then, it happened. The laughter burbled up from somewhere deep inside her, forcing its way from her lungs to her throat.

Nicole knew she was powerless to stop it. She never even tried anymore.

All heads turned toward her as the giggling sound she was known for came spurting out of her mouth.

"Okay, so did *everyone* see my green thong?" she asked the class. "Because, really . . . how embarrassing!"

TECHIES

Maggie tugged at the bottom of her over-sized sweatshirt.

She was fully aware that she didn't dress in the latest style. Anyone could tell, just by looking at her, that, in fact, she didn't subscribe to a style at all.

That was the point.

Maggie's brand of "fashion," while seemingly sloppy or even lazy on the surface, was a conscious choice. A wardrobe full of non-brands. A rebellion of baggy tees and sweatshirts.

If her mom would just stop leaving all those insipid teen magazines in her room, making subtle hints that Maggie should drop a few pounds or dress more trendy, maybe Maggie would do both.

But her mother's nagging wasn't the only thing

that made her choose the opposite. No, it went way beyond that.

She turned her head slightly to the right. Brittany Smith was sitting two rows over, painting her fingernails.

Maggie shook her head in disgust, but still, she couldn't stop looking.

She could never stop looking.

Thanks in part to those insidious magazines, she'd become obsessed with Brittany Smith's body, often studying how it folded neatly at the waist, creating the kind of angle they'd talked about in geometry. Maggie's stomach, by contrast, popped out slightly over the top of her jeans.

Was that it? she wondered. Was that the X factor? The indefinable, unspoken quality that made her worth less than Brittany Smith?

She *was* worth less—it was obvious. Somehow, she just wasn't as important in the eyes of her peers, her teachers, her own mother. Could it possibly be because of something as inconsequential as the shape or trajectory of her stomach?

Maybe it was her arms, Maggie mused. They, after all, were her fixation of the day. Brittany Smith's arms began a delicate curve somewhere between the shoulder and the elbow, ending in a tiny wrist the size of a toothpaste tube. Maggie's didn't. Her arms were white and fleshy—the same diameter all the way from her shoulder to her wrist.

Maggie's gaze traveled the length of Brittany's arm, then back up the incline of her body. She marveled at how narrow Brittany's torso seemed from the side, tucking itself neatly between two visible hipbones. Maggie's bones by contrast, were safely hidden under an ample protective layer.

Maggie leaned back in her chair, closed her eyes, and sighed. Why was this living, breathing skeleton universally worshiped—categorically revered by all the brainwashed morons around her?

She'd asked herself that question a million times. Maybe a billion.

Did the answer matter? Probably not. Definitely not in light of what Maggie had planned. Soon enough she'd embark on her mission.

It wouldn't be long now before she would *wake them all up*.

CHOIRBOYS

Ms. Howland was in such a mood. "You sound like wounded cattle!" she barked.

She never should have said that. The boys in the back row, who were only taking choir because they needed an elective, started mooing.

Perry Reynolds spun around. "If you're not going to sing, at least do everyone a favor and shut the hell up."

"*At least do everyone a favor and shut the hell up,*" Brad Calvert mimicked with a lisp, dropping his hand at the wrist.

"Okay, that's it." Ms. Howland sighed. "Looks like the back row needs a sectional. Everyone else sit in place. Back row . . . it's showtime!"

Perry dropped to his seat. He leaned to his right, into Christopher Jakes's doughy shoulder. "God, this is so lame," he whispered. "How long till we get out of here?"

"Not soon enough." Christopher's full lips twisted into a grin. "Unless you've got some extra-strength Midol for Howland, our torture continues for another half hour."

Christopher and Perry were close, but despite popular belief, they were not a couple. Even if they did experiment a little in seventh grade—back before either of them could admit that they'd be into each other.

Since then, Perry was aware that he'd never completely let go of his feelings for Christopher. But he tried not to think too much about it. After all, Christopher had moved on—a couple of times. It wasn't his fault that Perry was stuck in queer limbo.

"Howland hates those guys," Perry whispered, peering over his shoulder at Brad Calvert and the rest.

"Who *doesn't* hate those guys?" Christopher asked. "They're nothing but stupid muscle heads. Look at them! They can't even straighten their arms. They're like . . . *apes*."

Perry clapped a hand over his mouth to stifle his laughter. It was a struggle—especially while he was imagining Brad Calvert and his buddies in cages at the zoo, swinging on tires and flinging their own poop.

In his mind, Perry conjured a little plaque for genus and species information next to the jocks' cage: *Homo rejectus*.

The classroom door flew open then, rousing Perry from his daydream.

Christopher gasped. "Ooh—here comes my husband!"

Perry turned just in time to see Stone cruise into the choir room. He handed a call slip to Ms. Howland.

"God, he's divine!" Christopher breathed.

Perry rolled his eyes. "I guess. But why does he only go by one name? What is he, Cher? I mean, it's just so queer."

"Exactly!" Christopher whispered, gripping the sleeve of Perry's shirt. "He's latent. One of these days, he'll wake up and smell the testosterone, and when he does . . ."

Christopher began humming the wedding march in Perry's ear.

"Stone is *not* a closet fag," Perry scoffed. "I bet he just has a gay first name and doesn't want anyone to know what it is."

Ms. Howland took the call slip from Stone. "Well, what do you know?" she said, as much to the class as to herself. "It's for Brad Calvert. Brought to you by none other than . . ." Her hand swept grandly in Stone's direction. "A teammate." She shook her head and mumbled, "Off you go. I'm sure it's terribly urgent."

A small group of kids snickered, but Perry watched in silence as the object of Christopher's affection left the room with Brad Calvert.

As soon as they were gone, Christopher gave Howland the stink eye. "She needs to step off my husband."

"If Stone's your husband, then why are you seeing other people?" Perry asked.

"Placeholders," Christopher explained. "Just marking time until Stone realizes he wants me."

Ms. Howland pushed an annoyed, "Shhh!" between her teeth.

Christopher played it cool for a moment. But when Howland turned away again, his face collapsed into a scowl.

"That woman is on my last nerve," he whispered. "So, anyway. Wanna go get something to eat after school?"

Perry shrugged. "Maybe. Where?"

Christopher's broad smile sparked fear in Perry's heart.

"What now?" he asked.

"Nothing. It's just . . . I overheard Stone talking about meeting some friends downtown, and—"

"No. No way," Perry cut in. "Do you seriously have a death wish?"

"Hello? It's an ob-ses-sion?" Christopher knocked on Perry's bony forehead, once for each syllable.

Perry swatted his hand away. "Fine. Whatever. So where are they supposedly going?"

"Pommes Frites."

"Ugh," Perry groaned. "Do you know many calories are in one order of French fries?"

Christopher shrugged a softly rounded shoulder. "No. Nor do I care."

Perry lifted his shirt and pinched a handful of abdominal skin between two fingers. "Well, I guess I could have, like, eight."

"Yay!" Christopher quietly clapped.

Perry frowned. "Honestly, Christopher. I just hope you realize that the only person—the only one I'd *ever* do anything like this for—is *you*."

QUAD

"GET INSIDE!" RANGER SHOUTED again.

People were running faster and faster. Some pulled friends or strangers along with them as they ducked into any open door. Ranger stood and watched in disbelief. A flash of skirt ruffles. A streak of high-end gym shoes. Black and brown backpacks blinking past like strobe lights.

Expressions of fear and confusion flew by as he stood in the doorway of the student store.

Pages from the *Metro* fluttered through the air as someone stumbled over the rock that held them in place.

And then, in the chaos of the moment, Ranger saw something that seemed grossly out of context. Three girls, he couldn't quite tell who, strolling through the quad as if they were window-shopping at the mall. Though they seemed to notice the confusion all around them, the reason for it wasn't registering. Ranger could almost see a little cartoon bubble over their heads—read the words being typed inside, one letter at a time.

Omigod. Like, what's everyone geeking out about?

Jesus, Ranger thought.

"Hey," he yelled. "Get inside!" But they were too far down the quad to hear him.

"Get inside!" he shouted, watching as kids dove into nearby classrooms. He tried to remember the drill, the emergency protocol they'd practiced a couple of times a year. But he couldn't. He'd snickered his way through those drills, never really paying attention.

"Get the fuck inside!" he screamed again, waving his arms over his head.

By now the girls had stopped walking. They began gazing around the quad in puzzlement, surveying the chaos almost casually, as if it were an everyday occurrence.

Another *pop!* sounded without warning. Only this time it was louder.

Closer.

"Get inside!" he tried again, but it all sounded warbled in his ears, like he was yelling underwater.

He took a few steps out the door—toward them—but one of the jocks grabbed his arm. "Jesus Christ, man, what the hell are you doing?"

Ranger could feel everything around him slowing down: voices, movement. Time itself seemed to stop.

And then, as if a gust of wind had come up from nowhere, one of the girls' hair blew back, and in sickening slow motion, she crumpled to the ground.

TECHIES

Theo knew it was risky, hiding a video camera on his lap during a math test, but Mr. Aronson sat up front on test days, reading the paper and drinking coffee. Rumor had it that he spiked said coffee with something special he kept locked in the file cabinet. But that had never been verified, not even in the *Metro*.

Theo's intellect was known throughout school. He was well aware that he took a lot of crap for no other reason than his IQ. The teasing, the comments, the stares. The occasional beatings. That was why the steroid posse and those two preps who never shut the hell up pissed him off so badly. They were too cool to be smart, but they weren't opposed to taking grades they didn't earn.

Aronson only busted those kids who were openly cheating, but when he did, the bust was beyond humiliating—even those kids who had never cheated on *anything* felt guilty after witnessing one of Aronson's spectacular performances—so Theo knew he had to be careful. He positioned the tiny camera so that it was wedged into the waistband of his pants. He'd practiced, experimented, calculated the trajectory so that the lens would aim directly at the group of jocks and preps who always managed to cheat on the down-low and blow the curve.

Theo knew what he had to do. He knew those assholes were the ones responsible for the SAT fiasco. He fought to keep his face from flushing with rage as he adjusted the camera slightly.

Don't have a panic attack, he warned himself. *Just do what needs to be done*. He stroked his tiny camera and then pressed record.

"You will have forty-five minutes to solve twenty problems," Mr. Aronson droned, passing out the papers. "Do your own work, show your work, and turn your test facedown when you're done. There will be no talking. Begin." It was amazing how Aronson always timed his pre-test lecture to end just as the last paper was being handed out.

Theo made one last adjustment to the camera

and a spot check to be sure Mr. Aronson hadn't seen him before setting out to ace his test. All he had to do was tape and wait. Then he could give Stone and his little posse exactly what they deserved.

DRAMA QUEENS

PAISLEY REED STARED AT the poster on the door of the performing arts building. She picked at the peeling gray paint on the door as she read the flyer for the two thousandth time.

SPRING MUSICAL AUDITIONS
GUYS AND DOLLS

- BRING A FEW BARS OF MUSIC
- PREPARE TO DO A BRIEF READING
- DRESS COMFORTABLY FOR DANCING

Paisley sighed, fighting against the idea that she'd been defeated days before she even tried out.

She tried to tell herself it didn't matter—who cared if she had never made it into the school play before? This year could be different. *Guys and Dolls* could finally be her show. . . .

"Hey, chica!" Sage Wood leaned into Paisley from behind, clutching an armful of books to her chest. She smelled like warm skin and just a hint of BO. Paisley didn't mind. There was something comforting about it—it reminded her a little of her Grams.

"Hi there," Paisley said as they kissed each other on the cheek. The golden brown curls of Sage's hair tickled Paisley's nose.

Sage nodded at the poster. "You ready?"

"I dunno," Paisley admitted. "I get sick to my stomach every time I think about doing it."

Sage shook her head dismissively. "You'll be great." She stepped away from Paisley for a moment to assess that day's ensemble. Red swing skirt with white polka dots. White blouse with puff sleeves. Black shoes. White tights. And the hair!

Paisley knew it was the hair that put the outfit over the top.

"God, look at you! You're adorable!" Sage smiled. "I get it! You're Minnie Mouse!"

"Is it too much?" Paisley put her hand to her head, where she'd wound her dark hair into two buns and slid a red headband in front of them.

"Not at all," Sage insisted. "It's too cute."

A group of students walked by. One of them started singing "It's a Small World After All."

Paisley bit her lip. Sage didn't seem to notice the slight, or if she did, she pretended not to. "Come on," she said, linking her arm with Paisley's. "Let's have lunch."

The girls sat at a concrete table in front of the performing arts building—the same table they sat at every sunny day. On the odd rainy afternoon, they hid away in a corner of the library—except for that one time Paisley wanted to reenact the scene from *Singin' in the Rain* where Gene Kelly danced with the lamppost. Sage sat patiently at the table, getting soaked to the skin, while Paisley spun around a metal pole, singing.

"So, do you have your song ready?" Sage asked, opening her brown bag.

"Uh-huh." Paisley nodded.

"All right, then. Let's hear it."

Paisley cleared her throat. She would never do this in public. Not for anyone—not anyone, that was, but Sage.

Back in sixth grade, she and Sage had both ended up in Mr. Burke's class. Mr. Burke would later refer to them as "the inseparable Parsley and Sage." But on that first day of school, when he was taking roll, he'd called, *Paisley Reed*, and Sage, who was sitting right next to her, had turned and said, "Wow. Is that, like, a stage name?"

Ever since then, Paisley knew two things: she was meant to be famous, and Sage Wood would always be her biggest fan.

"Pais!" Sage said, her voice snapping Paisley back into the here and now.

Oh, yeah, she thought, *the song.* She took a deep breath and began to sing.

"Soooome-where . . . o-ver the raaaain-bow . . ."

Sage sat politely as Paisley made her way through two stanzas. The melody line was a little elusive, but all in all, she didn't think she was doing too badly.

A couple of boys sitting behind her giggled. One guy broke into an operatic falsetto as his friend snorted hysterically.

Paisley dropped her voice almost to a whisper and continued.

"Birds fly over the rainbow—"

More laughter from the boys nearby. Then a shadow fell across the lawn in front of Paisley.

God. Why couldn't they just leave her alone?

"Listen, you guys." She whirled around on them. Stopped short.

"Whoa. Sorry," Theo Martin said.

Paisley swallowed.

Theo, she thought.

"I didn't mean to interrupt." He had this slow way of talking. Hypnotic.

Paisley's face felt suddenly warm. Flaming. A vague smile pulled at the corner of her mouth.

"That was nice. Why'd you stop?"

Theo took another step toward her, and for the first time, Paisley noticed the video camera. It was no bigger than a pack of cigarettes. She looked up at him, her mouth open slightly.

"Is it this?" He shrugged, jerking his head toward the camera. "Sorry. I heard you singing and . . . I was wondering if I could tape you for this . . . this project I'm doing."

Paisley tried to speak, but her voice had dried up. She turned to Sage with wide, frantic eyes.

"You can film her," Sage told Theo. "Just not the singing. She's not ready to go public."

Paisley stared down at her shoes.

"Well, that's too bad," Theo said.

Paisley thought that even though he was frowning, in a weird way, it kind of looked like he was still smiling.

"Maybe I'll just catch you when the play comes out," he continued.

"The play?" Sage asked on Paisley's behalf.

"You know. The play." He motioned toward the

flyer posted on the door of the PAB. "The *Guys and Dolls* thing."

"Oh, yeah. The play," Sage chirped.

Paisley cut her eyes sideways toward Theo. He hesitated for another minute before taking one step to the left. "Well," he said—took two more steps. "See you guys around."

"Yeah." Sage nodded. "See ya!"

Paisley realized she was holding her breath. When Theo was far enough away, the air left her lungs in a *whoosh*.

She flopped onto the bench beside Sage, laid her head on her shoulder.

"Oh my God," she groaned against her warm skin. "I choked. I'm a complete idiot. You'd think I'd finally be over him. I mean, it's been like four years."

"I hope you don't mind that I turned him down," Sage said. "It's just—I could see how uncomfortable you were."

"Yeah," Paisley admitted. She watched as Theo moved farther into the quad. "You know, sometimes . . . I dunno, but sometimes I wish I hadn't dumped him."

Sage hugged Paisley close. As her gaze followed Theo, one of the seniors called to him from the student store.

"Hey, Einstein," the guy said. "Calculate the value of this." He held up his middle finger, and his friends fell over themselves laughing.

Paisley sat up, her eyebrows tugging together. "That is so mean."

She turned to Sage and shook her head. "Why do people have to be so mean?"

JOCKS

Brad Calvert would never openly admit it, but he kind of missed going over to Stone's house. It had this kick-ass rec room with a pool table, about a million video games, and a real pinball machine. It even had a full-sized refrigerator, which Stone's mom kept fully stocked with food and soda.

Now, of course, it was too damn depressing setting foot in the place.

Stone's mom wasn't around to cook for them anymore; his dad was always hiding out in the den, probably looking for mail-order brides on the Internet. Most of the cool stuff—the pinball machine, the pool table, the old rifle collection—was now in storage, tied up while Stone's parents' asshole lawyers fought over who would ultimately get what.

Calvert knew he *could* make use of his newfound free time by studying. He needed to bring his grades up so he could play again in the fall. He'd already been screwed out of a season of basketball, which . . . okay, sucked and everything, but if he got axed from playing his senior year of *football*? That would be the end of everything.

It wasn't like he didn't try. He honestly did. Even got a peer tutor to help him with homework and studying for tests. But the tutor was this totally hot girl, and all he could concentrate on was trying to nail her. Meanwhile his grades were tanking—worse than ever.

But honest to God, how could he keep his mind on school with all those girls running around? There was no enforceable dress code at Muir, so half the time there wasn't even anything left to his imagination.

So, yeah, it wasn't his fault. But he wasn't about to mention any of that to his dad, who would probably pull him out of Muir and ship him off to some heinous, all-boys military boot camp in Vermont or something.

I'd rather be a stupid jock, Brad thought, *than a stupid jock with no chance of ever getting laid.*

At least his dad was off his case about his SAT

scores. He'd pushed Calvert hard to take the damn test, even though Calvert knew he didn't have a chance in hell of going to a four-year college right out of high school. But it sure took the pressure off at home when Calvert came back with decent scores.

And it was all thanks to Stone.

In addition to being football captain, quarterback, and a damn good friend, Stone was a fucking genius. He was so smart, he probably didn't even *have* to cheat on the SATs.

But Calvert was sure as hell glad he did. That geek he earmarked and the plan he came up with? Pure genius.

After all, it got Calvert's dad off his ass—finally.

TECHIES

THEO RACED TO THE computer lab immediately after last period.

Most afternoons he spent either in the quad, taping, or in the computer lab, editing whatever he'd gotten on film that day. He set out to shoot specific things, like the jocks and preps acting stupid, which fortunately wasn't that hard to do.

On a *really* good day, he'd catch one of them doing something totally obnoxious, like blazing up behind the library or puking up the vodka they'd had for lunch.

Other times, he liked to film the fringe kids doing random stuff, like skateboarding down one of the only two stairwells on campus, because there was usually a spectacular wipeout about halfway down.

Theo grimaced. Sometimes, the facts of life at Muir were stranger than fiction. But there was never any shortage of scenes to tape because there was never any end to the drama.

That drama was part of what Theo resented so fiercely. If people would just shut the hell up and do what they came to school for, everyone might learn something—and no one would get hurt.

Too late for that, though, Theo thought. *Way too friggin' late.*

Someday, when the truth came out—when Theo got the chance to set his plan in motion—his videos would show everyone that there was no reason to feel sorry.

Not for the steroid posse, the jocks, the preps, or anyone he took down in the process. No, they'd all deserve exactly what they got.

Theo squeaked around the corner and into the lab. He could feel his blood pumping. He was sure he'd finally be able to nail all those kids in math class, to prove to Mr. Aronson that those assholes hadn't earned any of the grades he'd given them.

It wouldn't be near enough of a payback for what they did to him during SATs. But it would be a start.

He grabbed a blue cable from his knapsack, hooked his camera up to the USB drive on the computer, and pressed Play.

He sat back, pleased with himself. The angle was perfect. There were Stone and one of the girls—the giggler—in plain view. The other girl (Brianna? Brittany?) could only be identified by her hair, which was in some kind of weird updo. Theo had no doubt it was considered hip by pop culture standards, but personally he thought it looked stupid. The camera shifted slightly, and there was Brad Calvert too. In spite of the fact that he could only see Calvert's feet and legs off to the right-hand side of the screen, he could prove it was him by referring to Aronson's assigned seating charts.

Yes! Nailed it, Theo thought. At this angle, any note swapping, shoulder tapping, or whispering would definitely be caught on tape. He nodded his satisfaction, then opened a bag of chips and a soda. The cheating could crop up at any point during the forty-five-minute test period. He settled in.

Minutes ticked by. Only the crunch of chips and the occasional belch after a sip of soda broke the silence. He never let his eyes drift off the screen.

That is, until his chair took a hard, unexpected thump.

"Hey, watch it," he growled.

"Sorry."

The voice warmed him instantly, like pilfering a sip of his stepdad's beer when he was eight.

Theo looked up. It was her. *That girl.* He was pretty sure her name was Maggie. She came to the computer lab nearly every day—same time as he did. He instantly regretted snapping at her.

"No. I mean, that's okay," he rushed to apologize. "I was just . . . er, watching something."

"I can see that." Her smile pulled to the left. It was a friendly smile. How could she be so friendly when he'd just bitten her head off?

He looked at her, took her in. He'd never been this close to her—never been near enough to see the waves in her chocolate brown hair, the Caribbean blue of her eyes, and the smattering of freckles, constellations he had imagined the shape of countless times across the distance of the computer lab.

"So . . . what is it?" she asked.

He shook his head. "What? This? Just some stupid thing I'm working on."

"Oh." She blinked. "Anyway. I'm Maggie."

He stared at her for an inappropriately long time before breathing out one solitary word. "Yeah."

She smiled, blushed a little. "You're Theo. No introduction necessary."

He snapped out of his reverie. "What do you mean, no introduction necessary?"

Maggie let out a puff of cinnamon-scented breath.

"I'm sorry. I just—listen, can I hang out here for a minute?"

Theo paused. Thought about the angle on his video camera—about Maggie's request to sit with him.

Jesus, he thought, *is this my lucky day?*

QUAD

JESUS!

Ranger's heart was racing a million miles a second. *What the hell just happened?*

It didn't matter, he realized. He couldn't think. He had to act.

"Unplug that freezer," he told Davis and Calvert. "Unplug it and push it in front of the door!"

Neither of them moved. Maybe he was using too many syllables. He pointed at the chest-style freezer that was used for selling ice cream bars in warm weather. Two more pops sounded outside. Ranger felt a surge of adrenaline so powerful he could probably have moved the heavy box by himself.

"Move that chest in front of the door!" he barked. "Now!"

The jocks snapped out of their shock and into

action, hustling like they were on the football field at homecoming. The freezer was relocated in a matter of seconds, and then they stood in front of it, panting and waiting.

Everyone's eyes were on Ranger.

"What's going on?" Christopher asked. "What's happening out there?" He made a move toward the door, but Ranger blocked his path.

Just keep everyone calm, he coached himself.

"I don't know," he answered, shaking his head slowly. "It's probably nothing, but maybe we should just—"

"If it was nothing," Ken Davis interrupted, "why'd you make us come in here?"

"And what's everyone screaming about?" Maggie added.

"Listen," Ranger said, trying to stall the panic. "I don't know anything, okay? Just chill."

His eyes darted around the room, taking in the fear on everyone's faces. *They know something's up,* he told himself. *But they sure as hell don't need to know what I just saw.*

The longer he could keep it from them, the better.

"How can you tell us to chill?" Calvert demanded. "You herded us in here like freakin' cattle, man."

Ranger stood there, mute, unsure of what he should say.

"Those weren't firecrackers," Calvert said, "and I think we all know it." He looked around the room. "They were gunshots."

"Oh my God!" Maggie cried.

Several others gasped.

"Hey, shut up," Ranger barked at Calvert. "You're freaking everyone out."

"They should be freaked!" Calvert pointed toward the door. "People are shooting at us!"

"Shooting?" Sage breathed. "*Who?* Who would do that?"

"Oh my God!"

Everyone turned toward Christopher. He was standing on the countertop that ran along the perimeter of the room. He peered outside through one of the high, narrow windows.

"She's dead!" he cried.

"What?" Sage yelped.

"What are you talking about?" Ken asked.

Christopher's eyes filled with tears. "That girl. On the ground. She's—"

Pop!

Christopher's face contorted in sudden, shocking horror. He leapt off the counter and pressed himself flat against the floor.

TECHIES

MAGGIE LEANED FORWARD IN the chair she'd pulled up next to Theo's. The computer lab had some of the best chairs on campus, he thought. Padded, with wheels.

"So, I'll ask you again," she started, "what are you working on?"

"Nothing," he mumbled. "It's stupid."

Maggie laughed. "Really? Is that why you're in here every day? Working on something stupid?"

"Sort of." Theo shifted in his seat.

She was close. Too close. He could smell her hair. Some kind of flowery scent with a hint of spice. It made his knees feel wobbly. He wanted to shift back from her just a little, but—what if she took it the wrong way? No girl had sat that close to him on purpose. Not since . . .

He thought back. Junior high? How embarrassing.

Maggie tugged on the bottom of her fleece sweat-shirt. *Fidgeting,* Theo thought. Did that mean she was as nervous as he was?

He looked up, caught her watching the computer screen. He rushed to the mouse, clicked it off. Maggie blinked at the sudden disappearance of what was supposed to be nothing anyway. She turned to Theo, her eyes wide. Innocent.

"Are you making a movie?" she asked.

"Sort of," Theo repeated. His eyes met Maggie's— slipped right into them. He didn't usually do that— look people in the eyes. But those powder blue irises made it so easy.

"What's it about?" she asked.

"School," he answered awkwardly.

She leaned back in the chair, tipping her face up toward the ceiling as she rocked backward.

"School sucks." She sighed.

Theo nodded. "Yeah."

"Do you ever feel like you just . . . hate everyone?" Maggie asked, picking at the torn plastic laminate on the outer edge of the computer table.

"Yeah," Theo told her, trying not to stare. She looked nothing like those fake preps he despised. No, Maggie had a brain, real curves, and a soul.

He could tell already.

He was quiet for a moment, then ventured, "You ever feel like everyone hates *you*?"

Her lips twisted into a smile. "All day. Every day."

The answer caught Theo off guard. "Really? You seem . . . pretty nice to me."

"I *am* nice," Maggie mumbled. "But it's not like anyone would notice."

"Why not?" he asked.

Maggie tucked her legs underneath her, then spun her chair around in a circle. "Because I don't prance around with my boobs hanging out of my shirt—that's why no one notices."

Theo frowned. Was that what she thought?

Even worse—was that what she thought of *him*?

"That's got nothing to do with it," he argued.

"Four out of five horny boys would disagree," she said, giving the chair another spin.

Theo smiled at her, mostly because he didn't know what else to do. "What about the one who didn't?"

She grabbed onto the computer table and stopped hard. Her eyes locked onto his. "Who didn't what?"

"Who didn't disagree?" he whispered.

She shrugged. "Probably gay."

They stared at each other for a second, deciding if

it was okay to laugh. Way too many jokes had been made at *their* expenses—and they both knew it.

They simply smiled at each other cautiously.

Silence threatened to bring an abrupt end to their conversation, but Maggie jumped in. "So you're, like, really smart," she said. She placed a hand on Theo's arm. His heart slammed against his rib cage.

"Who told you that?" he rasped.

"I don't remember." She blinked. Once. Twice.

God, he thought, *those eyes . . .*

"So . . . *is it true?*" she asked.

He put his hand on the mouse, rubbed his finger back and forth over the wheel at the center.

She leaned forward, closing the tiny gap between them.

"Are you?" she asked again, barely whispering.

Theo swallowed hard. "Maybe."

"Then . . ." She drew the word out mischievously. "If you're so smart, why don't you show me what you're working on there?"

His finger hovered for a moment, touching down a couple of times. If he pressed hard enough, she'd see everything. Everything.

He clicked, and an image flickered onto the screen.

CHOIRBOYS

IT WAS ABOUT A five-minute walk from school to downtown. Perry couldn't believe he'd agreed to this. Idiot Christopher had been studying Stone's routine, learning what route he took between classes, where his locker was, when he used it, when he didn't. He'd also taken note of who hung out with Stone, how many jocks he'd have to take down (yeah, right) if he got caught stalking.

It occurred to Perry that that's exactly what Christopher had become—a stalker.

They were a full three minutes behind Stone and the steroid posse. Far enough back, supposedly, to appear coincidental.

"I can see it now," Christopher said as they hiked down Central, a light breeze rustling his brown curls.

"Me and Stone, lying in a meadow somewhere, covered in wildflowers . . ."

Perry rolled his eyes. "Should I get some highlights?" he interrupted so he wouldn't have to hear Christopher's ridiculous wet dream about Stone again. He ran his hand over his hair. "Or maybe some lowlights? I dunno. This blond part just seems a little brassy."

"A babbling brook somewhere nearby—"

"Okay," Perry interrupted, "you're being totally femme. You know that, right?"

Christopher's thick lips turned down at the sides. "Right," he snarked. "'Cause, 'brassy highlights'? Not gay at all."

Perry rolled his eyes. Christopher was doing the puppy pout.

"*God*," Perry groaned. "Do you know how many ways he'd kick your ass if he even *thought* you thought about him that way?"

"He wouldn't. Trust me. A boy knows these things."

Perry felt like he was about to gag.

"Did I tell you about this dream I had?" Christopher continued, his words coming out faster than usual. "We were at the prom, and I was making out with this mystery guy, and then I leaned back and opened my eyes and it was—"

"Look." Perry swung in front of Christopher, blocking his path. "I don't want to be your, like, buzz kill, okay? But I don't want to get my face pounded just because you can't be in love with a normal queer like everyone else."

Christopher's smile deflated. "But . . . Stone *is* a normal queer. I know it in my heart."

"For the last time," Perry said, "he's not gay. He just has a gay name."

Christopher slapped one hand against his chest. "Oh my God. You found out his first name? Tell me you know the unknowable!"

"No!" Perry swatted the side of Christopher's head. "It's a theory, okay? Just a theory. God!"

Perry swore he could hear the tension in their footsteps as they continued walking toward Pommes Frites. Huge poplar and oak trees lined the sides of the streets, their massive roots cracking and pushing up the sidewalk. Perry watched Christopher as he skipped over the jutting concrete and ran his fingers through overhanging branches. The hum of street traffic filled the dead air between them until a carload of guys whizzed by and one of them leaned out the window.

"Hey, ladies!" he called. "Need a lift?" The rest of the passengers brayed with laughter.

Christopher slowed down, nearly stopping altogether. Perry could see tears burning in his eyes as he asked, "Why do they have to do that?"

Halfway through ninth grade, Christopher told Perry that he had come out to his family and they were mostly accepting of it. He swore he would start tenth grade "out" to the rest of the world.

He wanted to be clean, he told Perry. He was tired of holding up the mountain of lies he needed just to make himself look "normal."

But Perry and Christopher both knew that the rest of the world was on defense when it came to them—as if they were some grotesque thing that everyone had to sidestep. Sometimes he and Christopher laughed about it, wondering how people could be so stupid. After all, they were the least offensive people they knew!

But other times—more often than not, if Perry was honest about it—it cut bone-deep. No one cared to know anything else about them once they realized Christopher and Perry liked other guys.

How totally minuscule, Perry often thought. *How small-minded for people to say hurtful things like that.* He wished, fantasized sometimes, that just once, someone would hurt those people back.

"Why do they think they can do that?" Christopher sighed.

Perry kicked a used condom into the grass as they walked past the plaza across from the restaurant. "They do it," he said as they crossed the street, "because they know they can get away with it."

DRAMA QUEENS

AT THE LAST BELL, Sage and Paisley walked
through the parking lot to Paisley's rusty old Honda.
Paisley reached into her bag to get her keys but
pulled out a Juicy Fruit wrapper instead. She'd kind
of forgotten she had it.

"Hang on," she said, plopping her bag and her
books into Sage's hands. She pealed the white skin
off the back of the wrapper, then pressed it, shiny-
side down, on her car door and scratched until all
the silver came off.

The girls stepped back. "There." Paisley nodded.
"The door's all finished."

She'd fought hard with her parents to give her a
car when she turned sixteen, and they finally
caved—sort of. They let her pick out the best car
that fifteen hundred bucks would buy. It was a

junker, for sure. But Paisley figured she could make it unique by painting the entire thing silver, using only chewing gum wrappers.

Paisley frowned. "I wonder how many more sticks it'll take to do the rest."

Sage shook her head, but she couldn't help smiling. "Why don't you just buy a whole case of gum and get it over with?"

"That would be cheating," she said, dead serious, adding as she unlocked the driver's-side door, "You have to do things in the right order." She climbed in, leaned over, and pushed open the passenger door.

As Sage folded herself onto the seat, she said, "Yeah, but at least you'd be done in this lifetime."

Paisley retrieved an insulated cooler bag from the backseat, opened it, and pulled out a Tupperware container filled with cheese cubes, grapes, and a packet of crackers, her after-school snack.

"Mouse food?" Sage asked with a smile. She adored Paisley's creativity, how she somehow managed to match everything to her outfit du jour. "You are too cute!"

But Paisley just nodded solemnly and took a bite of cheese.

"What is it?" Sage asked. She knew Paisley too well, could read her like no one else could. Something was wrong.

Paisley chewed and swallowed before saying, "You know . . . the audition. I just want to do a good job. Because, like, what if this is my last chance?"

Sage tipped her head to one side, studied Paisley's face as she popped another cheese cube and grape into her mouth. She knew how important it was for Paisley to do well in the tryouts, especially after so many failed attempts. But it wasn't really about the audition, Sage realized. No, there was a lot more to it. It was about Paisley's need to fit in.

It hadn't always been like this. For a long time, it had been enough for them to have each other. The dynamic duo, they called themselves. Only Sage knew the sad truth: that they were the friends no one else wanted. Sage was too sandals-and-granola for the popular crowd, and Paisley was just plain odd.

Sage wasn't sure when the dynamic duo had stopped being enough for Paisley. Ninth grade, maybe? Coming into high school? She had watched as Paisley tried and failed to be accepted into different clubs and organizations. And she was always the one to pick up the pieces when it was decided that Paisley didn't fit in.

But Paisley was sure that this time—*this* time—she had found her niche. She had a flair for the dramatic that she'd inherited from her Grams, she'd insisted. Although that flair had yet to produce a role—in even the chorus—of any of the school productions.

Sage gave her credit for never giving up when she herself would have stopped trying long ago. She knew there was no dissuading Paisley once she'd put her mind to something. All Sage could do was support her and stay out of her way.

Once Paisley was clear on who she was, Sage thought, there would be no stopping her.

CHOIRBOYS

CHRISTOPHER PUSHED INSIDE THE restaurant. Pommes Frites was packed. Perry counted at least fifty people in line ahead of them. He could see Stone, who was about the twentieth person back from the counter. Perry hated waiting in crowds like that, but he knew Christopher wouldn't mind. It would give him plenty of gazing time. Stargazing. Stone gazing.

"You're gonna get our asses kicked," Perry singsonged in his ear, struggling to appear nonchalant.

"Shut up," Christopher singsonged back, then cleared his throat and raised his voice to normal. "So. Do you know what you're getting?"

Perry shrugged. "I don't know. Don't they have, like, fruit salad or something?"

"Oh dear lord." Christopher rolled his eyes. "Please tell me you're not on a diet."

"I just need to drop, like, five pounds." He shifted his slender frame from one foot to the other.

"No, honey, *I* need to drop five pounds," Christopher insisted. "You, on the other hand, need to eat a sandwich."

"I just think if I tone up and do some highlights, that hottie at the gym might ask me out."

"Why don't you ask *him* out?" Christopher asked. Two or three kids in front of them turned, gave them the once-over, and sniggered.

Perry tried to ignore them. He frowned up at the menu board. "How come they don't just have a little side salad or something? I mean, what if I don't want fries?"

Christopher looked at him like he was insane. "It's called *Pommes Frites*. If you don't want fries, you go somewhere else."

"I *wanted* to go somewhere else," Perry snipped. "Remember?"

Christopher turned away, studying the menu board instead. "Ooh," he purred. "Rosemary garlic. Doesn't that sound heavenly?"

"Which do you think has more calories?" Perry frowned, rubbing his hand across his flat abdomen.

"French fries or onion rings?"

"Onion rings, for sure." Christopher nodded. "Because of all the breading."

"Yeah, but you only get like six onion rings as opposed to a hundred french fries."

The group in front of them snickered again and began elbowing each other. "Ooh," one of them said in a falsetto voice, "chili-nacho fries. Sounds heavenly!" Their laughter, which had barely been contained up till then, suddenly erupted and spewed everywhere.

Christopher looked at Perry, his soft features reddening with humiliation. Perry widened his eyes in response, tilting his head in a barely perceptible nod toward the door. But Christopher shook his head adamantly, practically digging his heels into the tiled floor.

Perry started to seethe. In ninth grade, when Christopher came out, he had actually written up and signed a contract that stated: *I will not let homophobia dictate my life or in any way prevent me from being able to go anywhere or do anything. I further acknowledge that I may, on occasion, have to stand up for myself in order to stand by my principles.*

Historically, Perry had not been quite so committed. And as they stood in tense silence waiting for their turn to order, he seethed with hatred toward the kids in front of them and with anger toward Christopher and his stupid contract.

I could write a contract, he thought. *It would declare: Whereas straight kids' lives are so easy, whereas they can hold hands whenever they want, kiss whoever they want (not to mention wherever they want), go to the prom with whoever they want, and whereas straight kids can even talk openly about their sex lives without fear of retribution (not even by teachers most of the time)—I hereby denounce my stupid friend Christopher, who prances around like his life as a fag is just as easy as theirs when it isn't. Freaking Pollyanna!*

Perry didn't notice that the steroid posse had already ordered until Stone walked by carrying a basket of curly fries. The lobby wasn't as crowded as when they first got there. Even so, as he walked past Christopher and Perry, Stone rubbed up against them suggestively.

No one else standing in line received that honor.

Christopher waited until Stone had passed and then secretly pinched Perry's leg.

Perry was stung by the look of undeniable glee on Christopher's face.

"You see?" Christopher nearly squealed. "Stone totally loves me!"

Perry was silent as Christopher ordered for both of them. They slid into their booth a moment later. As he reached for the salt, Perry eyed his friend, thinking he looked exactly like Maria from *West Side Story* just before she sang "I Feel Pretty."

Perry frowned and took a nano-bite of fry. "I don't think that nudge meant what you want it to."

"Bet me," Christopher breathed. "I'll never wash this arm again."

Stone's voice came over the wall of their booth. "Which arm?"

Christopher's eyes tripled in size. Perry felt the blood drain from his face. Neither of them moved.

Stone swung around the side of the booth, pushing himself onto the seat next to Christopher. "Which arm, faggot?" He picked up a squeeze bottle of ketchup. "You mean . . . this one?" He turned the ketchup bottle upside down and wrote *faggot* on Christopher's arm. "Guess you'll have to wash it now. Won't you?"

Laughter came through the divider of the wooden booth—from the other side, where the rest of the steroid posse was sitting.

Stone threw the bottle down on the table and stood to leave, but Perry beat him to it. He pulled his reedy frame up as far as he could, pretending not to notice that when Stone finally, slowly reached his own height, he topped Perry by nearly a foot.

"What?" Stone glared down at him.

"Wipe it off," Perry said firmly.

Stone's eyebrows arched up, wrinkling his forehead. A smirk pulled his mouth to one side. "I'm sorry?"

"He didn't do anything to you," Perry insisted. "Wipe it off and leave us the hell alone."

"Perry!" Christopher's foot shot out from under the table, knocked up against his shin.

"*Perry*," Stone said. "That's right. Perry the fairy— isn't that what they used to call you in junior high?"

Perry gritted his teeth. "*They?*" he challenged.

Stone feigned chagrin. "You don't think *I* would ever say anything so . . . so mean, do you?"

Perry's eyes locked onto Stone's. "Fuck you."

Stone sucked in a pseudo-shocked breath, then stage-whispered, "Well, I would, but little Christopher here might get jealous!" He pushed at Christopher's scalp with his beefy fingers.

Christopher let out a little yelp as his head flew sideways, hitting the side of the booth.

Perry could feel his blood pounding in his ears. He squared his shoulders.

"What are you gonna do, Stone? Beat him up?

That would be a little too obvious, wouldn't it? Like you're trying *too* hard not to look like a fag hag?"

Stone dropped all pretense of good humor. "Maybe I should bitch-slap *you* instead."

"Oh yeah? Let's go." Perry stuck out his chin. "I mean, if that's what you're in—"

He never got to finish the sentence. Pain exploded in Perry's face as Stone's fist connected. White star-bursts appeared in his vision. Blood shot up from his nose as if he'd just struck oil.

Son of a bitch. Stone had cold-cocked him.

Perry turned in time to see Stone's arm circle around toward Christopher, his fist coming in right under Christopher's eye. Christopher curled into the corner of the booth. His eye began to swell instantly.

A crowd began to gather around them, and the manager of Pommes Frites rushed over to see what was going on.

"We're done here," Stone said to the woman. "You can clean this shit up if you want."

The steroid posse marched out of the restaurant and down the street, leaving Christopher and Perry, crumpled and bloody, inside the greasy wooden booth.

CHOIRBOYS

CHRISTOPHER'S MOM WAS SURE to be home, so they decided to go to Perry's house. At least it would be empty there. It was always empty there, it seemed.

Perry's dad lived all the way down south, in a bachelor pad near the ocean. Since he no longer sent child support checks, Perry's mom worked two jobs trying to keep her son well dressed and well groomed.

He's sixteen now, Perry's dad had said on more than one occasion. *Nearly an adult. And if he chooses to live that kind of . . . lifestyle, well, he can buy his own goddamn clothes!*

What his father had failed to mention, Perry knew, was the real deal: His new girlfriend had a bit of a shopping habit herself, and dear old dad couldn't afford to keep two divas in up-to-the-minute fashions on a retired cop's salary.

Perry hadn't said a word the whole way home, just nodded when Christopher suggested they take an alternate route to his house. Perry knew that if things were different, Christopher would have filled the space between them with chatter. But now, to Perry's relief, there was only uncharacteristic silence.

Perry unlocked the door with a key he kept on a thin leather strap around his neck. His mom insisted that he wear the key like a necklace rather than carry it on a key chain. She was overly paranoid that he'd lose it or, in a more likely scenario, that thugs would beat him up, take it from him, and use it to break into their house.

Either way, frankly, there wasn't that much inside to steal.

Perry threw open the door, leaving Christopher to close it behind them. He beelined into the bathroom and began rummaging through the medicine cabinet for something to clean the blood off his face and disinfect the cut across the bridge of his nose. He was only mildly certain the nose itself wasn't broken.

He didn't care what Christopher did to tame the

angry shiner Stone had given him with one meaty punch. As far as Perry was concerned, that black eye was Christopher's own damned fault.

He leaned into the mirror, gently dabbed the blood away from the cut, wincing at the pressure. After a moment, Christopher ambled in and leaned sullenly against the doorjamb. Perry's eyes darted over to him for just a split second, but it was enough of an opening for Christopher to brave an apology.

"You were right," he said quietly.

Perry didn't respond, just wiped away the trails of blood leading down his lips and chin with a damp washcloth. He wondered how he'd hide his blood-stained clothes from his mother, since she still did his laundry.

"I should have listened to you," Christopher continued. "I should have been more careful."

Perry leaned into the mirror again and dabbed the cut with antiseptic cream. There would be no hiding that from his mom. He wondered what kind of story he could make up to cover for the injury. He couldn't tell her the truth— she'd be at school, demanding justice, and then she'd be over at Stone's house causing a scene with his parents.

Then, when Stone got back from his five days of

vacation (aka: suspension), he'd probably hunt Perry down and finish the job.

No, a story was definitely in order here.

"You've had crushes before, right?" Christopher asked, searching for any shred of empathy he could find, trying to pull Perry back onto common ground.

Perry shook his head. *You have no idea. . . .*

"You know that feeling, that being all . . ." Christopher wiggled his fingers in front of his softly rounded abdomen. "All swooshy inside. I can't explain it, but Stone just made me . . . he made me lose perspective."

Perry hunted in silence for a small butterfly bandage to pull the cut together while it healed.

"I know he's kind of a jerk." Christopher sighed, making one last, final appeal. "I just can't help being infatuated with him, you know?"

Perry turned his burning eyes away from the mirror and drilled them into Christopher's.

Even now, after all this? he thought bitterly. *Even after Stone humiliated us in front of all those people? You're still telling me you have a thing for him?*

He took in Christopher's puppy dog expression, made even more pathetic by the bruise around his eye, and he was suddenly clear as day about the answer.

Yes, even now.

And Christopher *still* had no idea how *he* felt.

Perry whirled away and scowled at his own reflection.

He stared—hard—into his very own eyes.

"Screw you," he said.

FREAKS

THEY WERE LATE FOR fifth period, but they'd both smoked enough bud over the years not to come to class stupid. Mrs. Miles could have blasted them for being tardy and disrupting class, but the truth was, Rufus was usually the only one who had done the reading—and was most always the only one who would, or could, answer her review questions. So instead of dressing them down, Miles gave them her "just-hurry-and-take-a-seat" look and continued calling roll.

The class was doing their daily journal write. Mrs. Miles had only two rules about that: nothing was off-limits and everything was confidential. She did, however, reserve the right to keep an author after class to discuss any entry she wanted. Rufus flipped open his notebook and began writing:

I will not come to class stoned I will not come to class stoned I will not come to class stoned I will not come to class stoned I will not come to class stoned I will not come to class—

He stopped, glanced at his paper, and nodded once, approving. Back when he was in the third grade, some stupid dodgeballer beat him up because his handwriting was "too girly." He began refining the art of sloppy penmanship after that. Now, in tenth grade, he had nearly perfected it.

He peered over at Ranger's journal. His entry consisted of two words: *Ranger Ng*. Sometimes Mrs. Miles called him Ranger Angst, but Ranger didn't get the joke.

According to Ranger, when his dad was born, the family name was Nguyen, the Vietnamese equivalent of Smith. But after his grandpa moved the family to the States, he shortened the name to Ng, which was pronounced "eng," to make it sound Chinese instead. Rufus once asked Ranger why his grandpa did that. He said was that it was because anti-Vietnamese sentiment was pretty high back in the seventies. When Rufus asked what that meant exactly, Ranger just shrugged and said, "I dunno. That's what my dad told me."

Mrs. Miles's voice interrupted Rufus's thoughts.

"Rufus, Ranger, come here, please." Her eyes darted to the two large windows that offered a picturesque view of the visitors' parking lot. "I need you to take this to Coach Tanner." She held out a slip of paper, which was folded and stapled shut.

"What?" The boys blinked their confusion.

"Hurry," she added, "he's waiting."

Rufus glanced out the window. Didn't see anything noteworthy. But still—

"That's, like, all the way across campus—" Ranger began, but Rufus elbowed him in the ribs.

"So, like, it might take a couple of minutes," he explained, trying to cover Ranger's moment of idiocy.

"It's all right," she assured them, her eyes darting again. "Just get moving. Now."

Rufus and Ranger recoiled as they walked out of the English wing, the brightness of the quad momentarily blinding them.

When their eyes adjusted to the sunlight at last, all they saw was the same old crap. A handful of kids out of class—hanging out on the lawn—the same faces every period.

It was mostly the jocks and cheerleaders—the student body elite. They were like free agents, with nowhere pressing to be, ever. A bunch of them were making posters for the upcoming rally and subsequent barbaric ritual known as varsity sports.

"Muscle heads," Rufus growled under his breath.

"Dude," Ranger snapped. "Be cool. You want to start some kind of fight?"

"Maybe." Rufus tried to kick a seedpod across the grass. Missed it entirely. "So, hey. Was that some kind of bud or what?"

Ranger looked over his shoulder at a group of jocks clowning around at a picnic table. "Christ, man, shut up! You want 'em to come kick our asses?"

Rufus snorted. "Dude, they wouldn't even listen to us if we were *talking right to them*. We'll be fine. We just have to stick to the story. Okay?"

"Right." Ranger sniggered. "Your locker got broken into."

Rufus nodded as they shuffled up the stairs to the gym. "Just keep telling yourself that," he instructed. "Tell yourself enough times and eventually it'll be true."

Ranger stared at Rufus admiringly. "Yo, that's deep, man. I gotta remember to write that down."

PE classes were in progress when they walked into the gym. Rufus took in the scene, which looked so alien, it might as well have been happening on another planet. Neither Rufus nor Ranger had been to gym class in a while. Not since a group of jocks told them they'd wipe the hardwoods with them if they ever got matched up for a class competition.

Since Rufus was a self-proclaimed Doughboy and Ranger a pacifist, and since the jocks had made good on similar promises in the past, the next-best choice was to simply stop going. Nobody said anything to either one of them about their absence.

As he crossed the gym floor, Rufus tried to ward off a weed-induced paranoia attack. He hated being here. The place *reeked* of danger—of jock. So he focused on something positive, like the way the hardwoods were polished to such a high sheen that he could see the reflection of his hair. He'd painstakingly braided it into dozens of little pieces the night before. It looked stupid cool.

"Hey, Ranger, why do you think Miles sent us here?" Rufus asked as assorted balls whizzed past his head.

Ranger shrugged. "So we could pass a note to the steroid posse's commander in chief."

"Doesn't that seem weird to you?" Rufus asked.

"Yeah, it does," Ranger admitted. "I thought it was just me, though. 'Cause, you know, I'm, like, pretty baked right now."

"Me too," Rufus agreed. They stopped in the middle of the floor, started to laugh involuntarily.

"Hey!"

One of the PE teachers had spotted them. Rufus and Ranger clearly did not belong in any gym, at any time, for any reason. She jogged in their direction, ready to dutifully kick them out.

"What are you two doing in here?" she demanded.

"We're looking for Coach Tartar," Ranger said, then broke into muffled giggles when he realized his mistake.

The PE teacher cocked her head, annoyance curling her lips.

"Tanner, dude," Rufus corrected. "Coach Tanner. For Miles. I mean, we have a note from Mrs. Miles for Coach Tanner." He nodded and smiled, pleased with himself for getting it right, especially under the circumstances.

The PE teacher pulled a radio off her belt and pressed the button. "PE-one to PE-two. Come in."

Rufus and Ranger traded smirks.

"PE-two," they could hear over the radio.

"Two . . . er, students are here to see you. They say they have a note for you from Susan Miles."

"Not expecting anything," Coach Tanner's voice crackled back. "I'm on prep, helping with the dogs up front. Can't deal with anything else right now."

"Ten-four," she said. "PE-one, out."

Ranger started to snicker again. Rufus elbowed him. Hard.

"Sorry," the PE teacher said, though she didn't sound the least bit apologetic. "You're out of luck for now. Come back later?"

"I don't think that's—" Ranger began, but Rufus punched him on the arm.

"Thanks," Rufus called to the teacher, backpedaling as he pushed Ranger out of the gym. "We'll do that. Thanks."

The moment they were outside, Ranger began to squawk.

"Dude, what the hell was that for?" He rubbed his arm where Rufus had hit him.

"Jesus, Ng!" Rufus threw his hands in the air. "Are you a total idiot or just a half-idiot?"

"Hey." Ranger winced at the insult.

Rufus shook his head in disbelief. He could hear the soft music of dozens of braids knocking together next to his ears. "You don't get it, do you? Miles sent us out here 'cause the dogs are up front, dude. She sent us to the gym to get us away from the dogs. *Capiche?*"

Ranger blinked in confusion.

"Let me spell it out for you," Rufus said, thrusting his hands into the deep pockets of his baggy pants. "Miles just saved our asses."

"Whoa, dude." A slow grin spread across Ranger's face. "Cool."

JOCKS

KEN LOOKED DOWN AND saw the metal weight bar, crossing in front of Stone's face.

"How much is on?" Stone asked.

Ken craned his neck to the side. "Two-oh-five."

"Add twenty," Stone huffed, readying for the lift.

"Are you sure? I mean, that's kind of a lot." Ken was much more cautious when it came to bench-pressing. He was more cautious when it came to *everything*, he thought. Which was probably why Stone was the captain of the football team—and he was still second string.

Yeah. Ken shook his head as he slid ten-pound plates onto each end of the barbell. Lack of caution. That was how a Neanderthal like Stone got a lot of things.

"Good thing I'm not a puss," Stone grunted as he adjusted his hands on the bar.

Calvert started laughing. "Hey, Stone, your mom could probably out-press—"

"Shut up," Stone interrupted. He locked eyes with Ken. "Is it on?"

Ken used his sleeve to wipe the sweat from his forehead. "Yeah. It's on."

Stone took a deep breath and in a single, fluid movement lifted the bar and pushed it up. Down. Up. His cheeks puffed out as he held the weights over his head.

Ken stood at the ready.

A few seconds later, he helped Stone lower the weight bar back down to the rack.

"Done?" he asked, his eyes darting to the wall clock. It was only three forty-five.

"Yeah, I gotta cut it short." Stone wiped his face on his T-shirt. "I promised Hayley I'd go home and study. She's worried I'm gonna fail math and not get to play next fall."

Ken winced as he thought of Hayley Banks with her soft brown eyes and her cute dimples. . . .

His own girlfriend had broken it off fifteen minutes after they'd arrived at the winter formal.

Dumped by one of the hottest girls at school.

Jesus. Ever since then, Stone kept telling him that he looked like a five-year-old kid lost in a grocery store.

Eat me, Ken would say whenever Stone teased him, and Stone would answer, *No thanks, but someone should.*

That's when Stone would look around for those two guys he called "choir fags." Once he spotted them, he'd elbow Ken in the rib cage.

There you go, he'd say. *I'm sure little Christopher would help you out of a jam.* Then he'd tip his head back and laugh for what felt like ten minutes straight.

Occasionally, Ken would force himself to smile along, but most of the time he just walked away.

"The thing is," Stone continued, "Hayley's folks are in Carmel, and her little brother's staying at an aunt's house or something, so . . ." He smiled broadly. "I don't know how much studying we're actually gonna do."

Ken didn't want to know any of the gory details. He liked Hayley—a lot, actually—and he didn't want to hear anything that would make him change his mind.

"So, you going to Massey's April Fools' party?" he asked, switching the topic.

"Probably. Bought a bag of smoke for the occasion," Stone said, pulling his tank top over his head. "You in?"

"Sure." Ken tugged his backpack on. "So you're, uh, not going to the game, then?"

Stone's brows knit together in confusion. "What game?"

Ken glanced up. "The volleyball game. *Hayley's* game. Her team's playing in that tournament?"

Stone scoffed. "No way. That's the same night as the party." He pulled a sock out of the toe of his shoe, smelled it, then shook it right-side out. "Anyway, I hate those away games. Not only do they suck in general, but there's nothing more depressing. I mean, *no one* goes." He started to pull the sock over his foot.

Ken shrugged. "You could go."

Stone paused mid-pull and stared at Ken for what felt like a minute too long. Ken tried not to squirm under his gaze.

"You need a girl, bro," Stone finally said. "Maybe you can hook up with someone at Massey's party."

"Yeah," Ken said. "Maybe."

And then, two thoughts popped into his head:

One: The girl I want isn't going to be at Massey's party.

And two: She's already with you.

PREPS

NICOLE MCCLINTOCK WAS STILL giggling a day later at cheerleading practice as she recounted the story that would have meant the end of high school for anyone else.

"I mean, can you imagine?" She pressed one hand against her cleavage. "The entire *class* saw my underwear. How totally humiliating!"

The girls around her tittered, a few even blushed, but the truth was, Nicole wasn't humiliated. Not even slightly. She enjoyed the attention. God knew, she had to get it somewhere.

Nicole had been addressing the cheerleading squad at large, but it was hard not to notice that her best friend, Brittany, was not hanging on her every word.

"Hellooo?" Nicole sang, waving her hand in front of Brittany's face. "I'm right in the middle of a story?"

"Whatever," Brittany answered.

Nicole reeled back in surprise. Was Brittany, like, on the rag or something? She began revving up for a major protest whine. Then she noticed—Brittany's gaze had that faraway look in it.

She was, like, bumming. Right in the middle of Nicole's story.

"What is it, hon?" Nicole asked, throwing her arm around Brittany's shoulders. "Tell me. I'll make it all better."

Brittany was mute. Her eyes ticked to the right. Nicole realized she was tracking something, or some*one*, across the quad.

Nicole followed Brit's line of vision. The volleyball team was leaving school, walking toward the bus that would take them to who knew what match—not that anybody cared. They were all dressed in their shiny, polyester brown-and-gold uniforms, kneesocks pulled to their full upright position.

The very sight made Nicole shudder. They were a giant, walking horde of fashion *don'ts*.

Trailing behind the team, identically clad in her own uniform, was Hayley Banks. She walked along with the rest of the players, her mousy brown ponytail bouncing behind her.

"Her?" Nicole yelped. "You've gone all Helen Keller over Hayley Banks? Why?"

Brittany hung her head low. "She's with Stone," she said.

"So?" Nicole asked.

Brittany sighed. "It's just . . . he's so hot, you know? And, like, I am too. And Hayley . . . I mean, Hayley's just a jockette-wannabe dyke. So why would he ever be with *her*?" Her whole face collapsed in a tragic heap, like she'd lost a diamond necklace or something.

Nicole stared at her a moment. "*Ohhh* . . ." she drawled. "I get it. So, like, the other morning? When he was playing grab-ass with you? You wanted it to be more along the lines of—"

Brittany nodded pathetically, practically falling onto a lunch table bench. "Oh my God," she groaned, flopping her head into her arms. "What on earth does he see in her?" Her words came out, muffled, from beneath her armpit.

Nicole sat on the bench next to her friend and rubbed her back in sympathy. She felt the all too familiar sensation of what Mr. Noriega called "righteous indignation." At least he did on the day Nicole refused to take a pop quiz in Spanish class. But anyway . . .

It wasn't fair that Brittany should feel this way, Nicole thought. Not when she had been there—had listened to Nicole's stories about her fat-ass white trash mother and how she cared more about Dr. Phil than anything going on in the real world.

No, Nicole decided, staring daggers into Haley Banks's back, *Brittany deserves better than this. And I'm going to make sure Brittany gets it.*

"Honey," Nicole said, gently sweeping Brit's hair behind her shoulders. "I think I've decided something about Hayley."

"What's that?" Brittany asked, lifting her head from the table.

"She's a lesbo." Nicole giggled. There was something about the word that sounded just so funny.

Brittany stared at her for a moment. "So?" she asked.

"So," Nicole continued, all sweetness and light, "if *you* expose Hayley as the hypocrite she is, Stone won't want anything to do with her. Then you can plant your flag in his mountain and claim him for the mother country."

Brittany's eyes widened in horror. "Oh my God. Have you been paying attention during history?"

Nicole rolled her eyes. "Track with me, Brit. You're cute, you're popular—God, you're a *cheerleader*. And what does Hayley do? Pulls her hair back in a ponytail, *with a huge scrunchie*, and chases balls around."

"I guess." Brittany groaned. "But they've been together for like *months*."

Nicole gave an exasperated sigh. "Well, I'm not

going to stand by while you wallow in self-pity like this. We have to do something to—" She dropped her voice to a whisper. "Shhh. Here she comes."

"Hey, guys." Hayley Banks lifted her hand in an awkward wave as she approached.

"Hey!" Nicole sang back. "Cute shorts!"

Hayley looked down, studied the oversized pants. "They're just for volleyball. There's a game tonight. I've got to be on the bus in a minute."

Hayley grinned. Nicole prided herself on her ability to make people smile. After all, she was a people person, great with the compliments, even if she didn't always mean them.

Hayley parked her foot on the seat of the lunch table and bent to retie her shoe. Nicole couldn't help but notice the fine blond hairs on Hayley's thigh, as if she stopped shaving at the knee or something. *Ew.*

"So, I saw your names on the prom committee list," Hayley continued. "I was thinking we could get together at lunch one of these days and start planning the theme."

Brittany groaned again. Nicole pinched her under the table, where Hayley couldn't see.

"We'd love to," Nicole said, and then forced out a little giggle. "So, of course, you're going to prom with Stone?" It wasn't supposed to be a question, but in the end it totally sounded like one.

Hayley stared at Nicole for a few seconds, then glanced around at the other cheerleaders.

Nicole narrowed her eyes at Hayley when she finally came back around.

"Of course," Hayley said flatly.

Nicole thought she detected a slight hesitation in her words, though. And she would know—she was great at reading people.

"S-so anyway," Hayley continued, "do you guys want to get together?"

"Sure." Nicole pulled her mouth into a smile. "We'll do that. Real soon."

"Great," Hayley said. "Okay, well. Just let me know."

"We will." Nicole waggled her fingers at Hayley. "Bye-e."

As soon as Hayley was out of earshot, Brittany whirled on her. "What the hell did you say yes for? I don't want to hang out and talk prom with *her*!"

"Stop bitching, Brittany," Nicole snapped. "I have a plan, okay?"

Laughter began to burble out of her lips.

"Just trust me."

JOCKS

HAYLEY BANKS SHADED HER eyes with her hand. The gym lights at Lewis & Clark High School were twice as bright as the ones back home at Muir. Maybe one of these days they'd actually replace all those burnt-out bulbs in their own gym. But for the time being, the principal just kept repeating the same line: Fluorescent tubes were expensive and money had run out for those kinds of "extras."

"Hey, Hayley," one of her teammates, Christy, called out. "Is that Ken Davis sitting up there?" She pointed to the highest bleacher on the visitors' side.

Hayley peered into the stands. The subject in question raised his hand and waved. "I guess so," she said. "What's he doing here?"

Christy shrugged. "I don't know."

Hayley held Ken's gaze a moment longer than she should have. She blinked, then waved back. "It's kind of sweet of him to come, though," she mumbled.

"Cougars!" Coach Betsy called out. "Huddle up!"

Hayley always felt a little silly calling her coach "Coach Betsy." First of all, the rest of the PE teachers at school went by their *last* names. But more than that, Betsy didn't seem like a grown woman's name. It seemed to Hayley that by the time a person hit twenty or twenty-five, she should graduate from Betsy to Beth. Or Liz. Or Penelope.

In fact, Hayley thought as she made her way to the huddle, *no one should be named Betsy . . . unless she's a cow.*

"Okay, girls," the coach pseudo-whispered, "Lewis and Clark's a tough team to beat and we've got an anxious crowd to please."

Hayley frowned at the stands. Was Coach Betsy on crack? There couldn't have been more than fifteen people sitting on the visitors' side. Even Hayley's own parents wouldn't have come to *this* game. They never came, unless she was playing right there at Muir High, right down the street from her house.

She brought her attention back to Betsy, forcing herself not to roll her eyes.

"We need to think defense tonight. Defense will be the key to winning this game. Okay. Team ready?"

"Go, Cougars!" the girls yelled on cue.

The volleyball game had begun.

* * *

A little over an hour later, Ken came down from the stands and made his way over to Hayley.

"Tough game," he said.

"Yeah." She sighed. "It'd be nice not to drop one every now and then."

Ken watched as she wiped sweat off her forehead with her wristband and then chugged half a bottle of Gatorade.

Heat radiated from her skin. He could feel it, right through his clothes.

"So . . . what brings you out here?" she asked.

"I don't know. Just bored, I guess." He punctuated the lie with a little shrug, hoping to make it that much more believable.

"Well, thanks," Hayley said. "It's nice to have someone in the stands. Stone doesn't 'do' away games."

Ken scoffed. "It's not like you're *away*, away. We're only twenty minutes from home."

"I know," she said, laughing softly. "Lame, huh?"

Ken shoved his hands deeper into his pockets. God. He hoped he hadn't made Hayley feel bad by stupidly reminding her that her boyfriend wasn't there. What the hell was wrong with him?

The rest of the team grabbed their bags and trudged, defeated, toward the gym door.

Ken rocked on his heels. "So, I guess I should—"

"Walk me to the bus?" Hayley asked. Brown eyes, the color of warm syrup, gazed up at him hopefully, rendering him utterly incapable of doing anything but nodding.

"Sure."

They strolled toward the parking lot in silence, their slow steps in perfect unison. Ken fought the urge to reach for her hand as they pushed through the double doors.

It was nearly dark out in the parking lot. Ken felt relieved to be away from the bright lights.

"I was just thinking, we've got another out-of-town game next week," Hayley offered. "It's a tournament. Would you . . . well, can you come?"

The hum of crickets followed her voice into the night. Before Ken could answer, though, Hayley steamrolled her own question.

"I mean, you don't have to. It was sweet of you to be here tonight and everything. . . ."

"Yeah, I don't . . . I don't know," Ken mumbled, praying she couldn't hear his heart pounding in his chest. "I'll have to check."

"Sure." Hayley half smiled. "Just, well, let me know."

They had stopped about fifty feet from the bus. The rest of the Lady Cougars were slogging up the steps and flopping into the vinyl seats. Ken could hear Coach Betsy begin her *that's-okay-you-played-great-anyway* lecture.

"So." Hayley looked around the parking lot. "I'm totally supposed to ride the bus home."

Ken's cheeks flared. "Uh-huh."

"It's just . . . if I have to listen to Coach Betsy's special *Go, Cougars* cheer the whole way back, I might hurl."

"Yeah, that would suck," Ken agreed, not knowing what else to say.

Moments ticked by in silence.

"Did you drive here?" Hayley asked.

"Yeah."

"Can I . . . I mean . . . would you drive me home?"

"Sure!" Ken blurted. Then he scolded himself: *Way too desperate.*

It didn't matter. Her smile lit him up.

"Thanks," she said, all dimples.

Ken stood, frozen with fear and promise, as the rest of Hayley's teammates clambered onto the bus.

"Everyone here?" Coach Betsy's voice echoed in the near distance.

"Not everyone," Hayley whispered. She grabbed Ken's hand, ducked, and ran with him to his car before anyone on the bus could see them.

JOCKS

KEN ROLLED THE WINDOWS down, thinking the breeze might help cool Hayley off. The weather had been so indecisive lately. Even so, it was an unexpectedly balmy night, unusually so for March.

"Thanks again for the ride. I'm glad you came tonight." Hayley sighed. "Even if we did get creamed."

"No big deal. I just like watching you play."

Ken glanced at Hayley out of the corner of his eye. His face burned, like that time in fourth grade when he got such a high fever, he began to have seizures.

"I mean, you played really well," he said.

"I played okay," Hayley conceded.

"No. Seriously. Like, you carried the whole team."

Hayley laughed softly, her dimples sinking deep

into her cheeks. "Slight exaggeration." She sighed again, leaning back against the headrest. Ken looked over and saw that her eyes were closed. He loved that she felt that comfortable with him—that safe.

His heart was racing as he barreled down the highway, fighting to maintain the legal speed. It felt like rebellion, having her there, so close to him. If Stone could only read Ken's mind, only know how many times he had thought about being alone with his girl . . .

Yeah. He'd bust a vein. Then he'd bust Ken's head open.

Team loyalty would only carry a guy so far.

"So, are you thinking about prom yet?" Hayley asked.

Ken swallowed. "Um. No."

She turned her head, opened her eyes. He could feel her looking at him in the glowing light from the dashboard. "How come?"

He shrugged. Then he heard Hayley sigh. "Look, Ken," she said. "Nicole McClintock wasn't worth your time."

Ken glanced out the driver's-side window. Shook his head. She had absolutely no idea. Maybe it was better if she didn't.

"Remember square dancing in PE?" Hayley

asked. "Remember the do-si-do? Well, that's how Nicole McClintock goes through guys, you know? Hand over hand, just like in square dancing."

Ken gripped the wheel tighter. "It still sucked," he mumbled.

"I know," Hayley agreed. "I mean, if you're going to break up with a guy, save it for after the winter formal, right? Have some compassion. I mean, who does that?"

I bet you never would, Ken thought. His feelings for her, nameless, confusing, strained in her direction.

Hayley turned in her seat, facing him fully. She leaned in close. "Can I ask you a question?"

"Okay," he said, immediately wishing he could take it back. Half of him would have told her anything at that moment. The other half wanted to pull the car over, open the door, and run far away into the night.

He felt completely lost, either way.

"What was it about Nicole that, like, attracted you to her?" Hayley continued.

Ken tried to shake the confusion out of his head. "You mean, what did I see in her?"

"No." She shifted on the seat, the vinyl squeaking against her bare legs. "I know what you saw in her.

The same thing *every* guy sees in her. But when you got past that, you know? What made you want to, like, *be with her?*"

Ken didn't answer for a long time. Though his body had recovered fully from the fever that took him down all those years ago, it sometimes seemed like his brain hadn't completely caught up. He choked too easily, was too often at a loss.

He breathed his apprehension deep into his lungs, then blew it out again.

"It was kind of an ego stroke, going out with her," he said.

"Wow," Hayley whispered.

"What?"

"I dunno. I guess that's just . . . that's pretty honest of you."

He could hear the disappointment in her voice—could hear it and couldn't take it. He had to make her understand.

"Do you remember fourth grade?" he asked.

Hayley smiled. "Yeah, we had Mrs. Anderson together."

"You probably don't remember this, but . . . I got kind of sick that year."

"I totally remember that," Hayley said, touching Ken on the shoulder. All the blood in his body rushed over to the spot, bubbling under the soft pressure of her fingertips.

"You were one of the nicest kids in class," she said, "and it sucked not having you there. There was no one else to just hang out with."

She paused. "I never really knew what was wrong with you, though. I just remember Mrs. Anderson saying you were in the hospital and you were really sick, and then we made you cards or something."

"Yeah." He cleared his throat. He'd come this far . . . should he keep going?

For years he had sworn that no one would know the severity of his condition. No one would call *him* lameoid, tell him to ride the short bus with the rest of the slow kids. He'd keep it a secret from everyone. 'Cause, shit—everyone had secrets. Right?

But he knew it would be different with Hayley. She had a heart.

Ken had seen it. Even when they were in the fourth grade, he was drawn to her kindness.

He'd known he could trust her all along.

"It was . . . it was this really high fever, and it kinda messed me up for a while. They weren't sure if I'd be, like, normal after that."

Hayley blinked, her mouth forming a soft, silent oval.

"I guess, for a while, I was afraid they were right—that I really *wasn't* normal. Going out with Nicole was, like, proving to myself that I turned out okay."

Hayley sat there, watching him.

Waiting.

What the hell was he supposed to say next?

She nodded silently. Then said finally, "God, I'm sorry. I had no idea."

"So . . ." He hesitated. Was it okay to ask her? He really wanted to.

"So, what did you see in Stone?" He held his breath for the answer.

Hayley did a half turn in her seat, moving away from him.

His heart sank. Maybe he'd pushed too far.

Hayley took in a deep breath and let it out very, very slowly. Then she whispered, "I'm not really sure how to answer that."

QUAD

"EVERYONE GET ON THE floor," Christopher yelped.

Before he could finish the sentence, everyone was flat on the dusty tile.

Ranger stared at the tiny crumbs and stray threads that littered the floor's surface. He watched the dust motes float through the air. It was like a whole land-scape down there—one that he could get lost in—until Sage broke the silence.

"Were those really gunshots?" she asked. "They sounded more like—"

"What else could they be?" Calvert snapped. "You don't have to be a genius to figure it out."

Ranger looked over at Calvert, studied him for a moment. He could see the same fear and uncertainty on his face as he saw on everyone else's; he was sweating the same sweat, would bleed the same blood if the worst were to happen. Why the hell did he have to be such a . . . ?

"Prick," Ranger grunted, not quite under his breath.

Calvert seethed. "Wanna come a little closer when you say that?"

"Shut up, all of you!" Ken hissed. "You're gonna get us killed."

The chatter died down for a few moments. Some of the kids squirmed, trying to find a comfortable position.

Everyone's eyes were on Ranger.

"What now?" Christopher asked.

"Christ, I don't know!" he yelped. "Why are you all looking at me? I'm not in charge here."

"You saw what happened," Maggie insisted. "That *puts* you in charge."

Ranger pressed his fingertips to his eyes, tried to push the memory out of his brain. *Fuck yeah, I saw it. Someone blew that girl away. Just friggin' blew her away.*

"Who was it?" Maggie asked.

Ranger couldn't answer.

Maggie turned. "Christopher, did you see who it was?"

He shook his head, wrinkling his forehead. "They were too far away."

The hippie girl, Sage, moved over next to him and put her hand on his shoulder. "I'm so sorry," she whispered. "You shouldn't have had to see that."

Ranger's entire body began to shake. He tried to control it, but there was nothing he could do.

"It was three girls walking around out there," he rasped. He turned to Sage to try to explain. "You know who I mean. Those girls. The ones who hang out with Stone."

"With Stone?" Ken Davis snapped his head in Ranger's direction. "Which ones?" he demanded. He looked like he was ready to pounce.

Ranger's mouth opened, but his voice caught in his throat.

"Which girls?" Ken repeated. He grabbed hold of Ranger's shoulders, shook them hard.

Ranger winced. "I—I don't know, man."

"Stop it!" Christopher shouted.

"Leave him alone," Sage yelled, inserting herself between Ranger and the jock.

Ken blinked, dropped his hands to his sides. His face went blank as he sank back to the floor.

"Jesus Christ," he whispered, his voice barely audible.

"Oh God . . . Hayley."

DRAMA QUEENS

It wasn't that Paisley was dense. She wasn't, but that didn't stop the other kids from making jokes about her "riding the short bus." It had more to do with the way she didn't always notice that people were making fun of her. That was what made her such an easy target.

She was sitting in biology, pretending to listen to a lecture on microorganisms, when a triangle of folded paper landed on her desk. She turned and looked at Sage, who was grinning back at her. Paisley picked up the note and opened it.

What did your mom say about auditions?

Paisley scribbled, *She said if I get another D, she won't let me do it.* She refolded the page and kicked it back across the aisle.

Sage frowned as she read the note. She scribbled something, then flicked it back toward Paisley's desk. But before it could reach its destination, a sandaled foot with French-manicured toenails came down directly on top of it. Paisley froze.

Nicole McClintock bent down, her boobs half falling out of a lemon yellow cami.

Paisley watched Nicole's shimmery hair fall to one side as she picked the note up off the floor. She had always imagined it would be a cinch to become an actress if she looked like Nicole. If you were that beautiful, you could do anything. You could wear a yellow cami in forty-degree weather and you'd never even feel cold.

"What are you doing?" Paisley whispered, trying to pretend she wasn't completely freaking out.

Nicole ignored her. She casually unfolded the note.

"Give it back," Paisley urged.

"Oh," Nicole whispered as she read. "I get it. So you're an actress?"

"Well . . . yeah."

"Are you in any movies?" Nicole asked, snapping a large, pink piece of gum.

Paisley felt her eyebrows squish together, giving her that confused look that kids often made fun of. "Um. No."

"Do you *want* to be in movies?"

"Yeah." Paisley sat up a little straighter, amazed that a girl like Nicole McClintock was expressing interest in her. "But, I dunno. It'll be really hard."

Nicole studied her for a moment. Frowned. "You mean, because you're just not pretty?"

Paisley's mouth dropped open. She closed it, then opened it again. Her vision blurred with unwanted tears, and she blinked like crazy to push them back.

She hated how easily people could make her cry, how red her nose and eyes would get when she did. Of course it was a good thing to cry on cue if you were going to be an actress. But as her mother often pointed out, Hollywood scorns a sensitive heart.

"Hey!" Sage leaned over and snatched the note out of Nicole's hand. "Give that back!"

"Hey!" Nicole squealed in surprise.

"HEY!" Mr. Edwards barked. "What's going on back there?!"

"Nothing," the three girls said in unison.

"You three. The enrichment questions from the end of chapter fifteen. On my desk by the end of the day tomorrow."

Nicole gasped. "But Mr. Edwards—"

"Yes, that includes you Ms. McClintock. Now take your seat." Edwards scowled for a few more seconds before turning around to the board to write *microor-ganisms*.

Yesterday he'd accidentally written *micro-orgasms*. Nicole had laughed long and hard—and wouldn't stop—until Mr. Edwards finally threatened to kick her out of class.

"Thanks a lot," Sage whispered. "You just had to butt in, didn't you?"

"Whatever," Nicole answered, throwing herself against the back of her chair. "Like, who cares any-way?"

Paisley stared down at the worksheet sitting on her desk. Fat tears dropped from her eyes, making big, wet splotches on the page.

She glanced up at Nicole.

Who cares anyway? she had said.

Sometimes, Paisley felt absolutely certain that no one cared.

No one at all.

FREAKS

THEY WERE SITTING ON one of the walkways, leaning up against the brick wall of the student center. Rufus was eating chili-cheese fries, and Ranger was most of the way through a forty-eight-ounce Dr Pepper.

Rufus used to give Ranger all kinds of crap about his caffeine consumption. "I bet Mountain Dew's a gateway drug," Rufus used to say.

Years later, they'd still laugh about it on occasion as they lit up a fattie.

"Man, I feel like I spent the whole week dodging juicers," Rufus said, stroking the foot-tall mohawk he'd fashioned that morning.

A can and a half of Aqua Net later, it was still holding up by lunch.

Ranger had once kidded Rufus that he should write the company. "Maybe they'll make you their new spokesperson," he'd said, choking out the words through the hair spray cloud hanging over the bathroom.

On the plus side, that hair spray *had* been a pretty good high.

"You're the one who said it would be worth it," Ranger argued, "and it was. I mean, that was the best weed we've ever had."

Rufus could see Ranger checking out his reflection in his cop shades. Ranger noticed a big zit on his cheek and pinched it to see if it would pop.

"Yeah, but don't you feel it, dude?" Rufus asked, an electric current running through him. "Like, tick tick tick tick tick. Any minute now, the steroid posse is going to come a-calling."

The possibility gave Rufus a sick thrill. Sure, the weed was gone, but Stone wouldn't hesitate to kick his ass anyway. It was the only response the steroid posse ever had to anything.

Bring 'em on, Rufus thought. Even if he did get beat up, it was the excuse he'd need to strike back at them harder. The reason he'd use to one-up them again.

"Seriously, dude," Rufus said again. "You don't feel that?"

"Maybe I'm too stupid to notice," Ranger said, looking at his finger to see if there was any pus on it. "I *am* half idiot, remember?"

Rufus winced. "Sorry about that, dude. But you were getting dangerously close to dense, you know? You were swerving into oncoming traffic."

"Yeah. That's chill," Ranger said.

Even though he'd never admit it, Rufus could see that the dig still hurt Ranger some. Maybe not a lot—just like a dull throb, like a bruise.

Rufus was scraping a fry along the plastic foam plate to pick up the tail end of some chili-nacho sauce and Ranger was slurping the last of his Dr Pepper when a shadow crawled, slow-mo, across their feet. They looked up in unison.

Ranger breathed an audible sigh of relief. It wasn't the steroid posse but Theo Martin, lumbering down the walkway in front of them. He was staring straight ahead, kind of robotically. Rufus and Ranger lifted a curious eyebrow at each other.

It suddenly occurred to Rufus that he and Theo were wearing the same pants: camo, oversized, with lots of pockets and zippers.

Maybe they weren't *exactly* the same, he thought as Theo crept past. Rufus's didn't have those little mesh windows in the pockets or the little red light that was . . . Wait a minute. What was that?

"Hey, dude!" he called. "Is that a camera in your pocket?"

Theo stopped walking, looking a little deer-in-the-headlights all of a sudden. He turned slowly in their direction. "What?"

"He said, 'Is that a camera?'" Ranger called.

Theo scowled and stomped toward them, glancing left, then right.

Rufus chuckled as Theo approached. He was wearing a T-shirt that read, *If you could read my mind, you wouldn't be smiling.*

Pretty funny, Rufus thought.

"Dude, you didn't have to yell," Theo told them.

"Sorry," Rufus apologized. "But whatever that is in your pocket? I think it's on. Is it on?"

Theo hesitated before answering. Rufus realized the only person who talked slower than him was Theo Martin.

"Maybe," he said. "Why?"

Crazy-ass Martin. He always had all kinds of techie shit in his pants and wires hooked up through his shirts and stuff. "The little red light is on, dude. I mean, if you're trying to go covert, it's not exactly working."

Theo grumbled something to himself.

"What're you taping?" Ranger asked.

Theo shrugged. "School stuff," he said. "People."

Ranger inspected his finger, then wiped it on the sidewalk. "Us?"

Theo grinned, his lips pressed together. The expression was almost . . . reptilian. "Maybe."

"What for?" Ranger asked just as Rufus was saying, "Is it for that big project in computer tech?"

Theo reached into his pocket and turned the camera off. "Naw," he said. "It's just for me. But, like . . . don't say anything to anyone, all right?"

"Sure," they agreed simultaneously.

"Who're you taping, though?" Ranger asked again.

That serpentine look returned. Rufus half expected Theo to hiss his next words. "Preps. Jocks. Assholes in general."

"Any teachers?" Rufus grinned, liking the video idea a lot.

"A few."

"Is anyone ever gonna get to see it?" Ranger asked.

Theo's gaze drifted out across the quad. "Someday," he told them. "When I'm finished."

QUAD

MINUTES TICKED BY. THE clock on the wall of the student store read 3:15.

We should all be leaving now, Ranger thought. *Me, Rufus, that girl lying out in the quad—we should all be going home.*

But the more that time wore on, the harder it was to believe that there was still a home—or any world at all—outside the claustrophobia of the student store.

He peered into the freezer case—pressed his face against the cool glass.

How long would the fruit pops and ice cream sandwiches last in there before they melted? he wondered.

Then he turned and gazed around the room. A parade of random thoughts ran through his head—

about the ice cream bars in the case, the people in the store, and how they were all the same—how they'd all start melting into nothing if something didn't happen soon.

How long would they all last? he wondered. Then he flinched. If Rufus were here, he'd slap him upside the head and tell him he *really* sounded like half an idiot.

Ranger could see the rest of the kids in the store straining against their captivity. A few began to pace like caged animals. The particularly brave ventured a glance out one of the high windows.

After a while, Christopher broke the silence.

"Who do you guys think it is?" he asked, keeping his voice at a whisper. "I mean, who would want to go around shooting people at the school?"

Calvert sighed, ran his hand through his hair. "Probably just some crazed homeless dude off the street."

"More like some jock having a fit of 'roid rage," Ranger mumbled.

"What did you say?" Calvert asked, his voice full of warning.

Ranger shrugged. "We all know you juice up for weight training. Isn't that stuff supposed to make you, like, homicidal?"

"You believe this freak?" Calvert asked Ken Davis. He feigned amusement, then pointed an accusing finger at Ranger. "You know what? I bet it's your side-kick. Yeah, your little trench coat friend. Where is he, anyway? Don't you freaks usually travel in pairs?"

"You have got to be kidding."

It was Maggie. Ranger turned to see her narrowing her eyes at Calvert.

"You *know* who it is," she told him. "We all know."

"No one knows anything," Calvert cut her off. "Freak here said it himself."

"You guys saw him at that party," Maggie pressed. "He was totally out of control."

"Jesus Christ, get off it!" Calvert shouted. "It's not him."

Christopher's eyes widened with fear. "But if it is . . ."

"If it is, it shouldn't come as a surprise," Maggie inserted. "Not to anyone in this room, anyway."

Ranger's head spun.

No, it wouldn't be a surprise. Not to anyone who saw what happened. Not to anyone who read the *Metro* or saw Theo's tape.

But they couldn't know — not for sure. Not until this whole thing was over . . . one way or another.

CHOIRBOYS

CHRISTOPHER HAD BEEN TRYING to talk to Perry since after the Pommes Frites incident. But Perry avoided him all day at school. And he wasn't answering the phone at home, either. Christopher had started dialing when he got home from Perry's on Wednesday, then again after school on Thursday. He called nearly every fifteen minutes after that until someone finally picked up the phone.

"Mrs. Reynolds? It's Christopher. Is Perry home?"

"Yes, he is," Perry's mom said. "He's up in his room, writing you a letter of apology."

"*What?*" Christopher yelped. "Why?"

"He said the two of you got in a fight on Tuesday. He said he gave you a black eye, and I assume that's where the cut on his nose came from. I must say,

Christopher, I'm terribly disappointed in you both. What in the world possessed you?"

"I'm sorry, Mrs. Reynolds. So, can I talk to—?"

"That was a question, Christopher. I couldn't get Perry to tell me, so I'm hoping to get the truth out of you. What could have caused such a horrible fight between you? You're best friends!"

"I . . . I don't think it's right for me to tell you, Mrs. Reynolds, especially if Perry doesn't want you to know. But honestly, the whole thing was my fault. We were arguing and I went to slap him and ended up scratching him on the nose, and he was just pushing my hand away in defense. I don't think he meant to hurt me. I'm sure he didn't. I don't think he should have to write me a letter, Mrs. Reynolds. I'm afraid if you make him do that, he might hate me forever."

Christopher heard Mrs. Reynolds sigh. He waited for what felt like a really long time before she said, "I don't ever want to hear about either one of you boys involved in something so violent again, do you hear me?"

"Yes, Mrs. Reynolds," Christopher promised.

Another, shorter silence followed. "I'll go get him," she finally agreed.

Christopher's heart did a nervous tap dance as he waited for Perry to get on the phone. It felt like an entire chorus line in his chest. He and Perry had never fought like this before. It would almost have been better if their story about hitting each other were true. Physical pain would have dulled much faster than the emotional damage they'd inflicted.

Because let's face it, he thought, *Perry is openly unsupportive of this crush, and I've been shoving it in his face.*

Christopher realized it was an insensitive thing to do.

"Hello?" Perry's voice, wary, came through the receiver. Christopher's heart leapt at the sound.

"Hey." Christopher found himself struggling to appear natural, heard his voice break anyway.

"Hey."

Silence weighed down the space between them. Christopher hadn't thought much about what he'd say beyond *hello*, mostly because he didn't think he'd have the chance to say anything else. In his mental scenario, Perry always hung up.

"I promised your mom I'd never beat you up again," Christopher said at last, hating the silence more than the awkwardness of a poorly timed joke.

"That's mighty big of you."

Christopher sighed. "I'm sorry. What else can I say?"

"Nothing. There's nothing you can say. Nothing I've ever said to you has changed your mind about Stone. Nothing I've said has made you step back and consider the situation clearly. Nothing I could possibly say will ever change how you feel about him. So what's the point?"

"I'm through with him."

"No, you're not," Perry argued. "You're obsessed—you said it yourself. You may not chase after him anymore, but you're not done with him. You just don't know how to leave well enough alone!"

"I'm done, I swear," Christopher insisted. "It's not going to be easy, I know, but . . . seriously, who do you think is more important to me, you or him?"

"Two days ago I might have said me. Today I'm not so sure."

"Come on . . . you don't mean that."

Perry scoffed. "Actions talk and bullshit walks."

"Perry!" his mother called from the other room. She didn't approve of him using that kind of language.

Christopher groaned. "What can I do to show you I really mean it?"

A long, slow sigh blew out of Perry's nose, straight through the phone line and into Christopher's ear. Christopher could hear the anger in that single breath.

When Perry finally spoke, his voice was full of humiliation and tears.

"You want to know what you can do?" he choked. "You can stop taking all of their shit. And next time—next time—you can stand up to them!"

JOCKS

"WHAT'S YOUR LOCKER COMBINATION, Doofus?"

A head full of idiotic braids bobbed upward, toward Stone.

"What for?" Rufus asked.

"Whaddya think?"

Stone had his crew with him as he set out to talk to the two losers whose PE locker he'd hijacked a while back. They were easy enough to find, sitting on a concrete bench under what Stone and his friends called the "freak tree." "You've got my stuff in your locker," he said, "and now I need it back."

The kid smiled—actually *smiled*—and closed his book. "So, how'd you get by without a cup this long, juicer? Not much there to protect, I guess."

Stone moved as close to Ranger as he could get.

"Your friend have a death wish?" he asked. "He need me to take care of that for him?"

Rufus flashed Ranger a look.

"No," Ranger whispered. He averted his eyes, fixing them on his Union Jack high-tops instead.

"Good," Stone said again. "Now gimme your combination." His eyes ticked over to Rufus.

Now that his folks had finally gone through every room of the house, taking inventory for the lawyers, his bedroom was a safe place to hide his stash again.

It made Stone nervous, keeping his weed at school. Coach had been hinting that the dogs were coming for another visit. And even if he wasn't the one who ultimately would end up in trouble, he'd be pissed off if he lost the whole bag.

"Like hell I'm gonna give you my locker combination," Rufus said.

"Then go. Open it. For me." Stone breathed the words right into Rufus's face. The rest of players crowded in on him, squeezing the air out of his lungs without actually touching him.

It was working. Stone could see it on the freak's face as his smug little smile faded away.

"Let's go," he added, his voice rumbling.

As they crossed the quad toward the gym, Stone smiled at the sight of Rufus and Ranger. Dead men walking. With four of the biggest football players marching behind them, the scenario could only have looked more ominous if they were pointing rifles right at their freaky little heads.

The locker room smelled like sweaty feet and bologna as the odd parade entered, rounded a corner of lockers, and screeched to a dead halt.

"Dude! What the fuck?" Stone shouted.

Rufus's locker was wide open, the door hanging lopsided on its hinges. Half of Stone's clothes were draped over the edge; the other half were in a rancid pile on the floor.

"My shit!" Stone swung on Rufus, who was twice as pale as usual.

The dozens of braids in his hair flailed wildly as Stone grabbed him by the front of the shirt and pushed him into the row of lockers. "Where's my stash, ass wipe?"

"Dunno, dude." The freak shrugged. He was keeping it cool, like he didn't feel threatened at all.

Stone gritted his teeth. He felt something hot surge through his body. Anger blurred his vision.

"I said. Where. Is. My. Shit?"

Stone cocked his fist. The freak narrowed his eyes in anticipation of the blow.

"Gentlemen!"

Stone let go of Rufus, pushing him forcibly away as Coach Tanner cruised into the locker room with a small entourage, including two dog handlers and a cranky German shepherd on a leash.

Coach Tanner looked confused. "Stone?" He frowned. "This isn't your locker, is it, son?"

"No, sir," Stone answered firmly.

"Then I need you to explain. Why did we find your jersey inside?"

Stone swallowed. Clearly, Coach Tanner didn't want to believe in any wrongdoing on the part of his players. All he had to do was come up with a reasonable excuse and—

"It's *my* locker." Rufus wedged himself into the conversation. Heads snapped in his direction as if no one had realized he was standing there.

Ranger's eyes darted above the tops of his just-for-show glasses. Rufus kept talking. "I haven't been using it much lately, so I told my boy Stone here that he could keep his extra stuff in it." He clapped a small, pale hand onto Stone's shoulder.

Everyone blinked, incredulous. Then Rufus added in apparent earnest, "The players have an awful lot of gear, sir."

Stone's jaw unhinged as Coach Tanner turned his full attention to Rufus. "The dog alerted on your locker, boy," he said, his tone changing quickly from paternal to authoritarian.

"Wow." Rufus nodded. Stone gaped—was this kid mocking the coach? "Did he find anything?"

Coach Tanner faltered for a moment. "Well." He cleared his throat. "No."

Stone shook his head, wasn't certain he heard right. The dog *hadn't* found anything? But how could that . . .

"Maybe he *alerted* on something left over from before." Rufus smirked. "I mean, just a thought."

Coach Tanner looked at the dog handler, who frowned, leaned in close. "He *can* detect some pretty minute residuals," the man whispered.

The coach stared at his players for a few uncomfortable seconds, then turned to Rufus and Ranger and scowled. "Fine. But I'm watching you boys. I'd better not catch you in any other trouble. Understand?"

"Yes, sir." Rufus gave a crisp salute. Then he and Ranger marched out of the locker room.

In that moment, it all became clear. The little freak had actually taken his stash.

And to make matters worse: He didn't even care if Stone knew it.

PREPS

NICOLE, BRITTANY, AND STONE all had Spanish together.

On game days, their teacher, popularly known as Señor Frog, didn't pay attention to the class at all. Instead he used the time to surf the Internet on his desktop computer. He'd set up an elaborate spreadsheet with the names and stats of every player on his fantasy football team and would busy himself during class plugging it all in.

Most everyone just chilled, read the latest copy of the *Metro*, or talked with their conversation partners for the period. That day, Señor Frog had picked some stupid drama queen to be Brittany's partner. It was Sage Wood, Miss Armpit Hair herself.

Nicole had been paired up with Stone. She was perched on top of the desk next to his.

While Brittany sulked on the other side of the room, not playing that day's version of "verb tic-tac-toe," Nicole saw an excellent opportunity to get the ball rolling for her best friend.

Moments like this, Nicole thought, were the reason that all the other girls looked up to her. No one else knew how to recognize a golden opportunity the way she did.

"Isn't it lame how he picks our partners for us, then couldn't care less if we play?" she asked, twisting a long strand of hair around her finger.

Stone ignored the question. "Aren't you cold?" he asked.

In a freak turn, the temperature had dropped fifteen degrees in less than a week. Not to be daunted, Nicole had chosen her tightest pair of low-rise jeans that day, tucked them into a pair of magenta suede boots, and slipped into a matching cami that showed off her new belly-button dangle. Then she wrapped a thick, fluffy scarf around her neck in a countermeasure against the cold.

"Cold? I don't think so." She giggled. "Everyone tells me I'm *hot*."

The emphasis had its intended effect. The other

students spun around and stared for a couple of seconds before turning back to their verb game.

"Anyway," she continued, as Señor Frog remained oblivious, "where's the party this weekend?"

Miss Armpit Hair left her desk and came over to use the pencil sharpener, which was right next to Stone's desk.

Stone shrugged. "There's one at Massey's, but not till after April Fools'."

"Oh, yeah. *Brittany* and I are going to that one," she said, running her flat-ironed bangs between two fingers. "Are *you?*"

Stone's eyes flickered over to Brittany for a second or two.

That's right, Nicole thought. *Brittany. Right over there. Get a good long look at what you're missing—*

"I dunno," Stone mumbled, turning back toward his desk. "Some freak stole a bag of weed I bought for the occasion, so what's the point?"

"Well, if *that's* the only reason," she said, picking up a pencil and doodling a *B* in the middle square of their tic-tac-toe sheet. "Me and *Brittany* can get some of her brother's Ritalin."

Stone kept on as if he hadn't heard a word. "Plus Hayley's got a tournament and won't be back in time."

"Sooo?" Nicole drew a circle around the letter *B*.

Stone frowned down at the paper. Nicole knew he was considering the possibility—was seriously thinking of coming to Massey's party without his butch girlfriend.

She turned her head and lifted an eyebrow in Brittany's direction. Brittany scrunched hers together.

"Why do you keep looking over there?" Stone grunted.

Nicole forced out a giggle. She needed to change the subject—quickly. "Have you ever noticed the way that drama queen over there is always staring at us?" She nodded in Sage Wood's direction.

"No," Stone mumbled.

"Maybe she thinks you're hot," Nicole suggested.

Stone leered. "Maybe she thinks *you* are."

"As if. I mean, she's not a lesbo, like—" She stopped short of saying "like your girlfriend." It wasn't time to reveal that part of her plan. Not yet. She needed to ease Stone into the idea—then strike when he was most vulnerable.

When he finally broke it off with Hayley, Brittany would so owe her.

Nervous laughter bubbled out of Nicole's mouth. Stone leaned back and closed his eyes for a few seconds. He raked his fingers through his coarse hair.

"Look. Just let me know if Brittany can get the stuff, okay?"

"Oh, totally. For sure." She smiled at Stone with two rows of perfectly white teeth. A moment later he got up from his desk, grabbed a hall pass, and walked out of the room. The door banged shut behind him.

Nicole giggled her way back over to Brittany.

Everything was going according to plan.

TECHIES

THEY WERE STANDING ON the top step of Maggie's porch. Behind her head, on the door, hung a kitschy floral wreath with a hand-painted WELCOME sign beneath it. At the bottom of the door frame, a little lawn gnome stood sentry, guarding the home, Theo supposed, from unwanted visitors.

He was sightseeing, he realized—and knew exactly why: He was a little afraid of Maggie's eyes, afraid if he went too far in, he'd never come back out.

After a week of hanging out in the computer lab, he was desperate for more time with her—more private time. Today, his devious though somewhat pedestrian plan had worked: stroll by Maggie's locker after school, marvel at the coincidence (oh, this is *your* locker?), and then gallantly offer to walk her home.

So far, so good. But now, Maggie hesitated.

"I guess this is where we say goodbye," she said.

"Maybe I could come in," Theo suggested. "See your room or something?"

Maggie's lips twisted into a scowl. For the first time since they began speaking, she seemed at a loss for words.

"It's okay if you don't want me to see it," Theo rushed, desperate to keep things cool. "I'd totally understand if you—"

"No," she blurted. "No, I—I want you to come in. But you have to swear to secrecy."

"Okay." Theo laughed. Even if he couldn't keep a secret, it wasn't like he had anyone to tell.

"No," she said, locking her eyes onto his. "I mean, you have to *swear*. To *secrecy*."

He tilted his head to one side. "Okay. So what do I—what do I have to do?"

She stared. Her eyes darted between his, searching for his hidden truth.

"Maggie?"

She studied him for a few more seconds, then leaned in and gently kissed him on the cheek. He stood there, dumbstruck, as she slowly retreated.

"What was that? Some kind of new age pinkie swear?" Theo asked, but Maggie just smiled in response.

"Maybe I should kiss you back," he added.

Maggie giggled. She ducked her head and turned toward the front door. "In my room," she said. "If you're good."

She took out her key, slid it into the lock, turned it to the right. She pushed the door open.

Theo wasn't sure what he was expecting to see, but inside, it was an ordinary house, not so different from his own. A blue velour couch with matching recliner in the living room, silk floral arrangements everywhere. Thomas Kinkade painting on the wall.

Modest. Humble, even.

"It's this way," she said.

"What is?"

Amusement tilted her lips to one side. "My room?"

"Oh, yeah. Right."

She took his hand, led him up the stairs and down a hallway lined with family photos. Theo stopped at a picture of an infant girl, presumably Maggie, in a bonnet with a wide smile across her face. He leaned into the photo; then he turned, studied her, tried to connect the dots.

"Pretty dorky, huh?" she mumbled.

His voice shot up an octave. "You were so cute!" He reached over and tried to pinch her cheek.

She knocked his hand out of the way. "Shut up!" She laughed.

Theo pointed to a small metal plaque at the bottom of the picture frame. "What does this mean, *Our Magnolia*?"

Her cheeks bloomed red. "That's me. My name—my real name."

"Magnolia," he repeated quietly. He loved the word, the way it sounded leaving his lips.

"What?" she asked, breaking him from his reverie.

"It's just . . . that's a cool name."

Maggie opened a door down the hall from where the baby picture was hanging. "You sure you're ready for this?"

Theo poked his head inside, surveying her room from a distance, as if it were a holy place. Sacred ground.

"You can come in," she offered with a smile.

He stepped inside and was surprised at what *wasn't* there. No stuffed animals, no girly things like makeup or jewelry, not a lot of clothes, no posters of teen heartthrobs. It was a tidy room, simple.

The walls were covered in corkboard, he noticed, instead of wallpaper. There were newspaper articles tacked up where posters of puppies and kittens might have been.

"So . . . what's the theme here?" he asked.

"What theme?"

"Don't most girls have, like, a theme for their room?"

"Do they?" she asked, a wicked smile lighting her eyes from the inside. "How many girls' bedrooms have you been in?"

"Well, I mean . . . Okay, it's just . . ." He choked. She was too intense, seemed to always know how to tie his thoughts into a knot.

Maggie took his hand, threaded her fingers through his. "I like to write," she said, her voice soft, low.

Theo's heart thumped in his chest. "So you, like, want to be a journalist?"

"I *am* a journalist." She moved in close; inches away, then centimeters. "Pinkie swear," she whispered, and kissed him with desperate urgency.

JOCKS

KEN WAVED TO HAYLEY from his seat at the top of the visitors' bleachers. Hayley smiled, waved back. The next game hadn't started yet, so she motioned for him to come down.

Ken hopped the metal benches two at a time and jumped onto the wooden floor.

"Hey." Hayley smiled at him, dimples deepening on either side of her mouth. She placed a hand on the side of his face. Ken's head spun. The gesture was so — intimate. There was no other word for it.

"What?" he asked.

Hayley shook her head. "Nothing. It's just . . . I like how your cheeks kind of . . . how they just kind of get red all of a sudden. It's cute."

"Thanks," he said, feeling his face grow hotter

than before. "So . . . are you still benched, or are you gonna get to play tonight?"

Hayley stole a glance at Coach Betsy, who was talking to the Stanton High coach across the gym. "I get to play. She's a total softie. I mean, she was pissed when she found out I didn't ride the bus home last time, but I gave her this major sob story about how my friend was having a crisis and needed a shoulder to cry on. She was even like, *Oh, honey, wanna talk about it? My door's always open*, and I'm like, *Uh, no, that's okay—that's why I went home with my friend, so we could talk*. But I told her everything's fine now."

"Wow. And she bought that?"

"Crazy, huh? She even promised not to call my parents."

Ken shook his head, still smiling. "So what was the big sob story?"

Hayley opened her mouth, but before she could answer, Coach Betsy called out to the team.

"Lady Cougars, huddle up!"

Hayley looked apologetically at Ken. "Gotta go."

"I'll be here." Ken watched as she started to jog away. "Hey . . . good luck!" he called after her, but she didn't seem to hear what he said. She just smiled back at him and shrugged.

Ken watched in agony with the eight or nine other people on the visitors' side as Stanton began steam-rolling Muir. It was nearly always a sure bet with the girls' teams that when they played away from home, they'd lose. Big time. Which was too bad, really, because they had a couple of pretty good players.

None of them can touch Hayley, though, Ken thought. *She's amazing.* He looked down at her just in time to watch her bump to Christie, then spike the ball just that side of Stanton's net. The nine or so people on the visitors' side gave a sad little "yawp" of excitement and a smattering of applause.

Hayley looked up into the stands as the team was regrouping and flashed Ken one of her amazing smiles. His heart nearly melted.

I don't know what I'm doing here, he thought. *But I'm a dead man. Or I might as well be, after tonight.*

TECHIES

THEO HAD NEVER MADE out with a girl before. He'd kissed his date good night after the winter formal last December, and for a couple of weeks in junior high he went steady with Paisley Reed. But this was different. This was lying-on-the-bed different. Theo thought he might be in love.

Maggie rolled onto her back and Theo flopped beside her. Taking a break was probably a good thing because at the moment, he was so turned on he could barely move.

"I really liked your movie," she whispered.

He shrugged, a little wary about having shown his video footage to her. "It's not finished yet," he told her.

"What do you mean?"

He frowned. "I still have a few scores to settle."

Maggie laughed. "Interesting choice of words. Is

that how you settle your scores? On film?"

Theo turned his head, reaching over to stroke Maggie's hair behind her ear. "You know a better way?" he teased. He decided to make his point by pulling his video camera out of his pocket and turning it on.

Maggie stared into the lens. "No," she said, unsmiling.

He leaned up on one elbow, focused in tight on her face. "No, what?" he asked. "You don't want me to film you? Or no, you don't know a better way?"

She kept watching him, her eyes burning into his viewfinder. "Maybe."

"Maybe what?" he asked, a little surprised.

She held her gaze on the tiny screen. "Maybe I have some scores of my own to settle. Maybe I have my own way of settling them."

Theo's heart sped up. "With who?"

She shrugged. "I dunno. Jocks. Preps. People who are out to get people like us."

Theo's head whirled. He was almost positive by now that he loved this girl. It was like she could read his thoughts—like they'd lived inside each other's heads their whole lives.

"Why are preps and jocks out to get *you*?" he asked, narrowing in on Maggie's intense eyes.

She blinked into the lens a few times. "Because they can't see beyond the package," she whispered.

Theo paused. What had started out as an amusing diversion was taking on an entirely darker dimension. He could sense something bubbling under the surface of Maggie's skin, a reckoning of some kind. He wasn't afraid of it; he actually wanted to explore it.

"What can't they see?" he asked, just above a whisper.

"Intellect," she said. "Heart. Soul. Danger."

"What kind of danger?"

Her hair fell forward, leaving only one blue eye visible behind a chestnut curtain. "The kind of thing that happens when they push too far without realizing."

Her face bounced a bit in the lens as he fought to steady his hand. Where was she going with this? he wondered. It all sounded startlingly familiar.

"What'd they do to you?" he forced himself to ask.

"It would take too long to tell you everything," she said, laying her head on her arm, still staring into the lens.

Theo panned out just a little. "Tell me the worst thing."

"The worst thing . . ." She blinked as she thought about it. "Once, at a dance in ninth grade, Stone came over and asked me to dance with him. At the

147

end of the song, he whispered in my ear, 'Thanks for dancing with me. Can I kiss you?'" She looked up at Theo, as if she'd just remembered he was there.

He was still filming—he wondered if she might ask him to shut off the camera.

"It's okay," he said softly. "Go ahead."

"I said yes because . . . I'd never kissed a boy before. And, like . . . it was Stone. Right? I mean, who wouldn't want to kiss the most popular boy in school?"

Theo's hand started shaking again. He panned out a little more, hoping it would mask the unsteadiness, but it didn't.

"So, did you do it?" He hated asking, but he knew he had to.

"I thought I did," she whispered. "He told me I had to close my eyes, so I did. But when I opened them—" She swallowed hard.

He gave her a few seconds to compose herself before asking, "Who was it?"

"It was Bernard," she breathed, her voice wavering.

Theo felt his blood boil. "Special ed Bernard?"

Maggie nodded bitterly. "I French-kissed Bernard the retard. In front of everyone. They laughed . . . and laughed. . . . They never stopped."

"Okay, so . . . how does a girl like you go about making something like that right?" He was probing her, testing her, making sure she was saying what he thought she was saying. Because if she was . . .

"Some of us settle our scores on film," she said. "And some of us settle them in print."

She rolled over and gazed up at an article tacked above her bed. Theo swept the camera in the direction of her gaze. There were newspaper articles hanging everywhere. . . .

He zoomed in on one—and gasped. Not just any articles—*Metro* articles. The underground school newspaper. It was . . . everywhere.

"You have copies of the *Metro* all over your walls," he said.

She continued to stare at him, blinking only once.

An unwitting smile cracked Theo's face. "Maggie . . . are *you* the one who puts out the *Metro*?"

"Remember. You're sworn to secrecy," she whispered, the softness of her voice at odds with the magnitude of her newly revealed identity.

Theo sat up, crossed his legs. His jaw hung open. "Why?" he asked. "Why do you—"

"Why are you making that video?" she countered.

Theo shut off his camera and eyed Maggie cautiously. He wanted desperately to trust her. But after all, what did he know about this girl? How did he know she wasn't just after a story—an exposé?

Then again, the identity of the *Metro*'s publisher was an unsolved mystery, Theo thought. What did Maggie have to gain by letting him in on her secret?

"Why are you making the video?" she whispered again.

Theo pushed away the tears of rage he still felt whenever he thought about it. The SATs—the way Stone's crew cheated off him, distracted him. Made him miss out on the full-ride scholarship he deserved.

He wasn't ready to tell her. Not yet.

"I've been working out a plan," Maggie said. "A way to really get even with those guys." She leaned into Theo, kissed him. "I think we could do an even better job of it if we worked together."

She moved her mouth to his ear, so close he could feel her breath on his neck. A shiver ran up his spine as she whispered, "So . . . care to join me?"

FRIDAY, MARCH 27

DRAMA QUEENS

THE THEATER WAS MOSTLY dark inside. Paisley caressed the black velvet curtains as she walked down the aisle that led up to the audience seating. It smelled like her Gram's closet in there: musty, almost wet, like maybe it had just rained. Paisley loved that smell.

Hot bright lights, covered in red and blue cellophanes, cast a purple hue onto the stage, and Paisley stood for a moment, trying to imagine herself under them. . . .

But she couldn't. All she could hear was Nicole McClintock in her head.

You'll never be in a movie.

You're just not pretty.

There were several groups of kids clustered

151

together in the auditorium, waiting for their turn to audition. They were the hard-core theater and music kids, the ones who practically lived between the PAB and choir room.

As much as she longed to be part of them, they were their own little world, like Oz, and Paisley had never learned the secret handshake or whatever it apparently took to get in.

Paisley was surprised to spot Perry Reynolds and Christopher Jakes there too. This wasn't their usual crowd. Every now and then, her eyes darted over to them.

Perry didn't seem to notice her, but she thought she saw Christopher smiling in her direction.

As she sank into a red upholstered seat, she began to wonder why she had decided to brave the audition alone.

"Can I come with you?" Sage had asked as they sat in Paisley's car a few days earlier at lunch.

Paisley was trying to grab a soybean with her chopsticks. It was harder than it looked. "I don't need an escort. I promised I'd go, and I never break my promises."

"I know, sweetie," Sage said. "I just thought you might like someone to—"

"I'll be fine," Paisley snapped. "I said I'd do it and I will."

Now, sitting in the shadows of the theater, Paisley was consumed by guilt. She had sent her best friend away and when Sage had asked her why, Paisley couldn't tell her the truth. Couldn't say what she suspected—that maybe Sage had been the cause of her bad luck so many times before.

That maybe Paisley was better off without her.

As she arranged herself in the middle section of the auditorium, she strained toward the group of true drama queens across the aisle from her. She couldn't quite pick out their whispered conversations, but she could sense a hushed puzzlement over her presence there.

A moment later, Ms. Howland and Mr. Jeffers stepped forward to introduce themselves. "As you all know, I'm Mr. Jeffers. I teach English and supervise the drama club. This is Ms. Howland, the choir teacher. We'll be conducting today's auditions." They gave a brief explanation of the process: first there would be the reading, then the song, and finally a short dance routine. "Everyone ready to begin?"

Mr. Jeffers called students out by name, and one by one the drama court took center stage. Comfortable and poised, they read their lines, hit each note, and landed each step in their dance routines.

Paisley prayed to the spirit of her grandmother for courage. Her grams had been an actual, real-live vaudevillian actress. If Paisley could just tap into that energy . . .

"Paisley Reed," Mr. Jeffers boomed.

Paisley's heart stopped. She clutched the arms of her seat.

"Paisley Reed," Mr. Jeffers repeated.

"Here." Her voice barely carried to the stage.

Mr. Jeffers frowned. "Are you auditioning today, Miss Reed?"

Paisley gulped. "Uh-huh."

He peered over the top of his reading glasses. "You'll need to come up here to do so," he said.

The other kids snickered. Even Perry and Christopher, it seemed, were caught up in the moment. It kind of surprised Paisley. It wasn't like they were her best friends; but even so. She stared at them momentarily, her eyebrows tugging together in confusion. But in the diffused light of the auditorium, they didn't seem to notice.

Paisley suddenly, desperately wished she had let Sage come. She had gummy legs when she stood up, all soft and wobbly. Teetering lightly, she inched her way to the stage.

Mr. Jeffers handed her a copy of the script, folded open to a specific page. She took it with a trembling hand.

"I'll be reading Uncle Arvide and you'll read for

Sarah Brown," he said. "Start at the arrow."

Mr. Jeffers cleared his throat. "*And I never saw until now how much in love with him you are.*"

Paisley scanned her line. "*I'll get over it,*" she whispered.

"*Why would anyone want to get over the one thing you hope for from the minute you're born and remember until the day you die?*"

The line repeated. Paisley gave it a little more force this time. "*I'll get over it.*"

"Why?" Mr. Jeffers recited. "*Because it's the greatest reward that woman or man can have on this earth? To love and to be loved?*"

Paisley felt goose bumps quiver up her arms. *To love and be loved.* Wasn't that all anybody really wanted? The line left her breathless. The page swam before her eyes.

"Ms. Reed? It's your line," Mr. Jeffers cued her.

Paisley swallowed against the sob burning in her throat.

"Ms. Reed," Mr. Jeffers repeated, annoyance creeping into his voice. "Are you finished?"

Yes, she realized. She *was* finished. Finished before she'd even started.

She handed Mr. Jeffers her script and bolted from the auditorium.

CHOIRBOYS

CHRISTOPHER AND PERRY SAT quietly in the fourth row of the PAB, listening to the plan in the works around them. While Mr. Jeffers and Ms. Howland were huddled in a corner, making a show of selecting the cast, the members of the drama club were hatching a scheme to shut Paisley Reed down, once and for all.

"She's just embarrassing herself, auditioning here every season," Christopher heard someone insist.

He looked over to see who it was—Jenna Gray, the girl predestined for the role of Sarah Brown. "Someone needs to teach her a lesson. We'll just copy over the list, make a few changes, and post it."

"Don't you think someone's gonna notice?" Austin Emerson asked.

Austin—Mr. Lead Role himself. Christopher

knew *he'd* never get a lead role, and neither would Perry. They were only there because Mr. Jeffers was desperate for male cast members and Ms. Howland had offered extra credit to any boy in choir who auditioned.

"Who's gonna notice?" Jenna challenged.

"Like, Jeffers and Howland?" Austin argued.

"Why would they look at the list after they post it?" Jenna asked. "They already know who's on it. They knew before we auditioned."

Christopher surveyed the faces in the group, saw the clandestine grins, the looks of unspoken collusion. And then he noticed the shadow of a smile, sitting just inside the corner of Perry's mouth.

"Are you going along with this?" he asked.

Perry shrugged. "Better her than us," he whispered.

FRIDAY, MARCH 27

JOCKS

"COME ON, STONE, CONCENTRATE." Hayley pulled her ponytail through an orange hair band. "You need to know this. It's going to be on the test."

Stone scoffed, running his eyes over Hayley's body. She looked pretty cute in those tight workout shorts. He couldn't remember what attracted him to her first. Was it her ass? Maybe. But there was also something about the way she made him feel. Like he could be, just, better around her.

"I'm not worried," he said.

"Well, you should be," she told him. "If you fail—"

"The thing is," Stone said, snaking his arm around Hayley's waist, "I don't fail." He dove toward her neck. "I'm an excellent test taker."

Hayley shoved him away. "No, you're not. I know how you 'pass' your tests, Stone, and it isn't right. Now come on—tell me the square root of—"

Stone didn't want her to finish the question. He rolled her onto the bed and tried to kiss her.

"I'm not going to do anything with you," Hayley huffed from under the weight of him, "until you tell me the square root of—"

Stone sat up sharply. "Jesus, Hayley, come on. It's been a rough week. Everyone's been breathing down my neck—first the dogs, then my parents. I mean, can't you give me a break?"

Hayley eyed him warily. "Yeah. What about that thing with the dogs? I mean, you promised you weren't using anymore."

"I'm not!" Stone yelped. "I mean, I told you I wouldn't, didn't I? It was one of those little freaks trying to set me up." He folded her in his arms, pulled her close to him, nuzzled her hair.

Hayley stiffened. Stone could feel the smile fade from his face. "You believe me, don't you?"

She stared at him for a few seconds before getting up and padding across the floor. "Maybe studying in my room wasn't the best idea after all. Too many distractions."

There was a sinking sensation in Stone's stomach. "Hayley, come on. It's not like you're my paid tutor. You're my girlfriend. And we haven't spent any time together."

She was standing at her bureau now, moving

some small figurines around on the top. She scoffed, muttered something, then looked over her shoulder at him.

"I'm worried about you, okay? If you don't bring your grades up, you'll get kicked off the team. You'll lose your chances, you'll lose your friends, and then you won't have anything to—"

"I'll still have you," he interrupted.

She stared at him, silent. He could feel a sense of dread rising to the surface of his skin.

"Hayley . . . ?" He wished his heart would stop pounding. He was afraid she could hear it in his voice. "Are you saying you'd break up with me for . . . for getting bad grades? For not playing football? For—what—being a *loser*?"

She swung around. "That's not what I'm saying."

Stone's stomach clutched. He turned his head away from her, blinked quickly to keep the tears from coming.

She moved back toward the bed. Took his hand. "All I'm saying is, I'm here. And I want to help you. God, Stone . . . let me help you."

He stood, grabbed his jacket, and headed for the door. If he didn't get out of there, he'd lose it for real.

Hayley said she wanted to help, but Stone knew, more and more each day, that it was too late.

No one could help him anymore.

DRAMA QUEENS

Sage didn't care how many times it took: She'd call Paisley's house until someone finally came to the phone. The Reeds didn't have an answering machine—Paisley's parents considered them an intrusion. But Sage knew that, eventually, someone was bound to answer.

Come on, Pais, she urged inside her head. *Come on—pick up!*

Off. On. Redial.

"Hello?"

"Mrs. Reed?"

"Yes?"

"This is Sage." She waited for an *Oh!* of recognition. There was nothing.

"Sage Wood?" she added, just to be sure.

The silence wound itself around Sage's head as

she thought, there was no doubt which side of the family Paisley's oddness descended from. And then, finally, Paisley's mother spoke. "What can I do for you, Sage?"

"Is Paisley there? I'd really like to talk to her."

"She's sick."

Sage frowned. That didn't sound right. She had just seen Paisley earlier in the day. "What do you mean?"

"I mean, she's not feeling well." The words crackled through the line. "I don't think she's up to coming to the phone."

"Okay, but . . . this is kind of important. I mean, really important. Could you just—"

"I don't think so, Sage," Mrs. Reed interrupted, taking a swift bite out of her question.

"But I have some good news." Sage paused, confused. Why would Paisley's mother want to keep them from talking? "I think it might help cheer her up."

"Is this about the tryouts you pushed Paisley to do?" Mrs. Reed asked, and suddenly it made sense.

Paisley's mom blamed *Sage* for the audition disaster. Which was fine, since she'd blamed herself too, at first. But now . . . now everything was different.

"It's really good news," Sage said again, "and I think she'd want to be the one to tell you."

Mrs. Reed sighed. "Hold on. I'll go see if she's up for a chat."

Sage felt her heart beat faster as she waited for Paisley to come to the phone. It seemed like an agonizingly long time before she heard a muffled, "Hello?"

"Pais?"

"Yeah?"

"Honey," Sage blurted, "they posted the list this afternoon."

There was nothing but quick, shallow breathing on the other end of the line.

"Paisley? The list?"

"What about it?"

"Honey, you got a part."

"I did?"

"You did!"

Paisley squealed. Sage could hear her laughing on the other end of the line, then crying, then laughing again.

"See," she told Paisley. "I knew you'd have your time to shine."

QUAD

THE SOUND OF SHUFFLING feet, just outside the building, shut down the conversation inside.

Ranger's eyes, wide with fear, tracked the sound around the perimeter, from the back of the store to the front. He watched as the knob on the door turned to one side, then to the other.

"Oh my God," Christopher whispered frantically.

Ken held a finger up to his lips. *Shhh!!*

The doorknob turned again, quicker this time, like whoever was on the other side couldn't quite believe that the door was locked. Then . . .

Knock.

Knock.

It was quiet but firm.

Knock knock knock.

"Shit," Ranger breathed, not loud enough for anyone to hear.

"Anyone in there?" the person on the other side of the door whispered.

Tears spilled onto Sage's face. She grabbed Ranger's arm.

"If anyone's in there, open the fuck up!"

Ranger looked over at Ken Davis.

Stone? he mouthed.

Ken nodded.

"Let him in," Calvert whispered, his face turning bright red.

"*No!*" Sage barked.

"Hell, no!" Ranger agreed. "Are you crazy?"

"You can't," Maggie insisted. "It's him. *He's* the one with the gun."

"No way," Calvert insisted. "You're all insane."

"God, I'm so sick of this!" Everyone turned and stared at Sage Wood. "You all know it's Stone," she whispered. "He has no conscience. He picks on everyone. He beats people up for no reason." She glanced at Christopher, who was staring open-mouthed, with one eye that was still partly black and blue underneath.

"There isn't one person in this room he hasn't hurt," she finished.

"Sage is right." Maggie nodded emphatically. "It *is* Stone." Her eyes darted around the circle of faces, searching for consensus. "You all saw what he did at Massey's party. You saw Theo's tape. He's a walking hazard."

"Who's in there?" the voice from outside called, a little louder this time. "I can hear you. I know someone's in there! Goddammit, let me in!"

Ranger shuddered. This time, there was no mistaking it. It *was* Stone—just outside the door.

"Don't do it!" Maggie turned toward Ranger. "It's a trick!"

"What trick?" Calvert scoffed.

"You're not supposed to let *anyone* in," Ranger said, a split second from the school's emergency drills popping into his head. "Once the door's locked, you're not—"

"What," Calvert cut in, "you're not supposed help anyone else? It's tough shit for everyone who gets left out there?"

Ranger nodded. "Actually, yeah. I mean, what's he still doing outside anyway? Why didn't he come in when all those people were screaming?"

"Because it's *him*," Sage insisted.

"Jesus Christ, open the door!" Stone begged. "Please, help me!"

A growing cloud of suspicion hung in the air as two distinct camps began to form inside the student store.

And as the lines were being drawn, Stone continued to pound from just outside the door.

TECHIES

MAGGIE ALWAYS WORE HER backpack backward. It was a lame attempt, she realized, to cover up what everyone could plainly see: that she was fat. Still, it felt safer being able to clutch the bag against her chest, like a shield. She imagined it would ward off an attack, verbal or otherwise, should the need arise.

But today, as she'd walked home, her arms were wrapped tighter around her book bag than usual. Because her head was buzzing with thoughts of Theo.

She'd had such a crush on him since the beginning of freshman year, and now she was thinking just *maybe* she stood a chance with him. She almost wouldn't let herself believe it.

Maggie let herself in her front door, ate a snack,

then went straight to her room. She lay on her bed for hours, just thinking. She had no idea how long she stayed like that, dreaming about Theo. It wasn't until she sat up again that she realized it was well into the evening.

She rolled over, walked to her computer, pressed the button, and waited for it to hum to life. She cued up the footage Theo had given her so far and continued to upload it onto their new Web site.

Maggie smiled. In a few days, *this* would be the most trafficked page in the history of high school.

It was a good sign that Theo had trusted her with the files, she decided. A lot of it was pretty intense—embarrassing, sometimes damning images of everyday life at Muir High. She loved those parts of the film.

But she'd also noticed something else—something that disturbed her. There seemed to be an inordinate amount of footage of Theo's ex-girlfriend, Paisley Reed. Those clips were softer, almost tender. They were definitely out of step with the rest of the video. If Theo was planning on using the film for a "greater purpose," the way they'd agreed, Maggie couldn't figure out what all that footage of Paisley was doing in there.

Unless . . . unless, of course, he still carried a torch for her.

Maggie's stomach tightened at the thought. She'd never stand a chance against a girl like Paisley—tall, slender, artistic, eccentric. The kind of girl she imagined a guy like Theo would be into.

Paisley Reed, Maggie realized, could be a problem.

She frowned as she clicked off the Web site and switched to her publishing software.

It doesn't matter, she told herself. *I'm a clever girl. I can think of a way to keep Paisley in her place.*

She double-clicked on the *Metro*'s latest issue. Waited as the file opened.

After all, she had the tools right at her fingertips.

JOCKS

THE METRO

written, edited, and distributed by anonymous

DRUNK AND DISORDERLY

Muir High School preps, athletes, and cheerleaders have been committing widespread "PUI"
(Posing Under the Influence) and getting away
with it. No venue is too big or too small for the
PUI trend: parties, classrooms, the quad; some
have been spotted Posing Under the Influence
at school functions, like sporting events, even
while participating in them.

Teachers, administrators, and coaches, who
sources confirm have all been trained in recog-
nizing the signs of substance abuse, seem to turn

a blind eye to this issue, as if these particular student groups are simply untouchable. Drug dogs target the lockers and cars of known or suspected "stoners" (see Dog Day Afternoon, page 4) while overlooking some of the worst offenders on campus.

"Hey, Stone," Brad Calvert shouted across the weight room. "Check this out." Calvert handed Stone the issue of the *Metro* he'd found on top of his locker that morning. Stone began reading aloud:

Football captain "Stone" has kept his true identity hidden since—

"Dude, what the fuck!" he blurted, crumpling the paper in his hands. Calvert, however, wouldn't let it go. He snatched the balled-up rag. A crowd began to form around him as he continued reading.

Football captain "Stone" has kept his true identity hidden since he moved here in junior high. *Metro* sources have revealed, however, that Stone's real name is . . .

"Stop, Calvert," Stone warned. "I mean it."

Calvert looked up, snickered. "Stone's real name is *Harold*."

A roar went up from the locker room. The entire team celebrated Stone's unmasking.

"Shut up," Stone told them.

But his teammates continued to hoot and holler. "Haaarooold," they chanted. "Haaarooold!"

Stone felt a wave of anger wash over him. That wasn't *his* name, damn it. It was his father's. And he wanted nothing—*nothing* to do with that pathetic little shit!

Calvert kept on.

Harold Stone, Jr., is often affectionately referred to as "Stoner," and sources add confidentially that it's not just an endearing nickname. *Harold* has been known to be the "entertainment provider" for many of Muir's post-game parties.

Another cheer from the crowd, this time, more approving.

Not that it mattered to Stone. It did nothing to ease his mind. Someone had crossed the line. Not just crossed it, pole-vaulted over it. And that person was going to have to fucking pay.

How long will this PUI trend last? Most of the students surveyed for this article say: indefinitely.

Stone closed his eyes as the red-hot wave washed over him. His entire body thrummed with rage. He wanted to hurt someone. Really hurt them—maybe then someone would understand the way he felt.

Calvert glanced over at him. "You look pissed."

He grabbed Calvert by the collar, shoved him against the lockers.

"Dude!" Calvert yelped.

The unexpected arrival of Coach Tanner took everyone by surprise. "Listen up," Coach said, all business. "Because I'm only going to say this once."

Stone let go of Calvert's shirt. He turned his back on the other players and stared at the row of lockers.

Coach paced the aisle, surveyed the faces that circled him. "I do not condone drug use of any kind in my players. Not prescription drugs, not street drugs. Not performance-enhancing drugs. Is that clear?"

The players nodded, glancing alternately at their shoes and at each other.

"I said, *is that clear?*" Coach barked.

"Yes, Coach Tanner," the team snapped their response.

"And anyone who gets caught with drugs of any

kind . . . is off the team. Is *that* clear?"

Again, the players responded in unison, but the words stuck in Stone's throat. He spun the combination of his locker. He threw open the door and began gathering his books. He took a cursory glance up at the top shelf.

It was empty.

Jesus Christ—the canister. Where was the creatine he—

Stone felt his stomach sink. He leaned his forehead against the cool metal door, fixed his eyes on the *Metro*, crumpled near his feet on the floor. He shook his head. Tried to make the rage inside him disappear.

Without warning, the toes of Coach Tanner's shoes moved into his line of vision.

"Stone." Coach clapped a hand on his shoulder. "I'm going to need to see you in my office, son."

DRAMA QUEENS

THE METRO (P. 3)

THE SCUM'LL COME OUT . . . TOMORROW

Auditions are now taking place for this year's spring musical, *Guys and Dolls*. We all know who will try out, and we can be equally assured of which drama queens and choir fags will garner a coveted role (see the regular school paper, the *Gold Pan*, for that lame article). It's no surprise, either, who will *not* be selected for this fine cocurricular. It's difficult not to notice, for example, that no jocks go out for the play; no brains go out for the play; no preps go out for the play; no freaks or stoners would be caught dead even leaning up against the outside wall of the theater building. No, none of these kids try out because they are fully aware that they are not welcome in the inner sanctum known as the PAB (performing arts building).

In which case, the real story lies in why drama-queen wannabe Paisley Reed is on this year's roster when everyone knows that the casting is predetermined.

Only the power elite of the PAB ever wins these prestigious roles, yet Miss Reed, who is always the bridesmaid but never, ever the bride, is now miraculously on the list. Did she suddenly sprout talent after years of failed attempts? Or is it, perhaps, the mother of all April Fools' pranks? Insiders have confirmed that legitimate cast members created a phony list and posted it on the door of the PAB. So . . . the joke's on you, Paisley Reed! Happy April Fools' Day!

Sage found a copy of the *Metro* on her chair in first period. Her heart pounded as she flipped through the pages. The names of the articles alone were enough to make her sick. "Drunk and Disorderly." "Come Out, Come Out, Wherever You Are." She couldn't stop herself, couldn't help reading it. It was so destructive, like watching a car accident, yet being powerless to stop it.

Her eyes burned as she turned each page, but it wasn't until she read the story about the school play that her heart started to race, and the tears pushed in.

Oh my God, she thought. *Paisley. I've got to keep this away from her!* She wasn't sure how anyone could go a whole school day without coming across the ubiquitous "underground," but she was resolved to take whatever steps necessary to ensure that Paisley didn't.

Paisley had been so depressed after leaving that horrible audition. And making the cast was the shot in the arm she'd desperately needed. If Paisley saw this awful article, it would be the worst thing imaginable.

Sage knew it was her responsibility to protect her. Paisley would never have done that humiliating audition if it hadn't been for her. This, all of it, was her fault. And now she had to, somehow, make it right.

She tucked the paper into her bag and asked the teacher if she could use the rest room. Once outside, she scouted the area looking for as many copies of the *Metro* as she could find.

She could take them all and destroy them, she

determined. Throw them into the recycling bins in the teachers' workroom, shred them in the principal's office—whatever it took to keep them out of Paisley's fragile hands.

She had just spotted a stack of undergrounds outside the C wing and was scurrying over to get them when she saw Paisley coming out of the girls' rest room. Her eyes and nose were bright red.

She was too late.

Sage dropped the pile of papers on the ground. "Oh my God!" She rushed up to Paisley. "Oh, honey, I'm so sorry."

Paisley fell into Sage's arms. "It's so mean," she sobbed. "Why do people have to be so mean?"

MONDAY, MARCH 30

CHOIRBOYS

"OH . . . MY . . . GOD!" CHRISTOPHER tried
not to hyperventilate. He fanned his face with a
trembling hand. "Oh my God, oh my God, oh my
God . . ." He fumbled for his cell phone. He was
shaking so hard he could barely type the text mes-
sage he wanted to send to Perry.

Did u see the metro?

Christopher was sitting in science class while Mr.
Edwards was lecturing on the microbe du jour.
Someone from the previous class had left a copy of
the *Metro* on his chair.

Perry had Foods that period. Christopher was
more than a little jealous because every day they
cooked something fabulous in that class. Christopher
was a total pushover for gorgeous food. Not to mention what a waste Foods was on Perry, who left class

every day saying things like, *I wonder how many calories there are in a melon ball.*

Christopher's phone vibrated. He was surprised to get a reply so quickly.

No, why?—ptf

Christopher furiously pushed buttons. Perry had been referring to himself as Perry the Fairy ever since the Pommes Frites incident, knowing full well that Christopher hated it.

Stop saying ptf. Did you see the news?

The reply came back immediately.

???

Christopher looked around, made sure that Edwards was still droning on before he continued.

Go get a metro

Five minutes later, a call slip arrived for Christopher. It was from Perry—he recognized the handwriting. Friday, Christopher watched in awe as Perry swiped part of a pad of call slips off Ms. Howland's desk. She was too busy disciplining the back row in choir to notice.

At first, he swore he'd only use them for dire emergencies, but just two periods later, he reversed course.

"Why should Stone and the rest of the steroid posse be the only ones who attend class at will?" he'd asked.

"Because," Christopher breathed, "*this* is against the rules. It's dishonest!"

Perry fixed him in a strange gaze. "So?" he said. "I thought you liked that in a guy."

* * *

THE METRO (P. 5)

COME OUT, COME OUT, WHEREVER YOU ARE

And what mediocrity awaits us this year, direct to you from the PAB? Why, it's *Guys and Dolls*, that contemporary and timely musical about a Salvation Army virgin (not something most Muir High School students can relate to) and a bunch of gambling addicts. The protagonist finally gets drunk and throws herself at her seducer (we're getting warmer. . . .), and in the end, the audience comes away with a backpack full of squeaky-clean morals and values. If there were any true talent at MHS, the show might be worth sitting through, but alas, real talent is not to be found at MHS, which means the drama freaks and choir fags can offer us no such hope. The only thing we're left to do is re-name this year's yawnapalooza: *Gays and Dulls* and hope for something more entertaining—like watching half the cast come out of the closet!

"Jesus," Perry said as soon as Christopher came outside. "You're right! This is so incredibly unacceptable! We have to do something about it."

"Unacceptable?" Christopher's face registered surprise. "I think it's kind of fantastic." He peered at the underground paper Perry was still holding in a trembling hand.

"What do you mean, fantastic?" Perry snapped. "This article is bullshit. I mean, they're calling us *fags*. Christ—when is enough enough for you?"

"What are you—"

"God, Christopher, don't you get it? Once again, we're the target of someone's hatred!" He shook his head at Christopher's apparent confusion. "I mean, I assume that's why you texted me?"

Christopher looked at the upside-down title, "Come Out, Come Out, Wherever You Are," like he'd never seen it before. He shook his head. "No, not that!" He pulled the *Metro* out of Perry's hands and flipped to another page. "This!" He pushed his finger at a completely different article.

Perry could barely make out the article through his tears as Christopher tapped the page emphatically. There was a look of pure, unadulterated satisfaction on his face as he spoke.

"His real name," Christopher enunciated precisely, "is Harold!"

JOCKS

AS SHE LEFT PRACTICE, Hayley saw Stone sitting on one of the concrete benches near the gym. His hands were clasped between his knees, and he was staring off into space.

"Are you guys done with weight training today?" she asked, sitting next to him, but not too close.

"Yeah, I am," he said, his eyes darting away from her.

She studied his face as they sat quietly on the bench.

"So why are you still here?" she asked.

"What's the point in going home?" he mumbled.

Hayley sighed. The trouble, she knew, was Stone's dad. Stone blamed him for his mother's departure. "You can't keep avoiding him," she said.

"I'm not avoiding anyone." Stone's deep voice rumbled, slow and deliberate, toward her. "There's nothing to avoid. My mom's living the life she always wanted, and my dad's locked in his office, licking his freaking wounds. It wouldn't matter if I went home or not, that's all."

She placed a hand on Stone's shoulder. "They tried, Stone. They tried to make it work."

"Really? Who tried?" he asked, raking his hand through his short hair. "The only thing they did was drag my ass to this podunk town in junior high so they could 'make a fresh start.'" He tried to laugh, but it fell flat. "Some start. He let her screw around on him, and I did everything I could to not be a part of their bullshit."

"Like change your name?"

"I didn't change my name. I just shortened it." Stone let out a sharp breath. "Christ," he mumbled. "Naming me after him was the last manly thing that bastard ever did. How's *that* for irony?"

Hayley watched as Stone fought to keep his face from contorting. Sometimes she wished he'd just cry and get on with it. She knew he had a lot of conflicting emotions bottled up inside him, but she was terrified of what might happen if he didn't let it come out.

"Coach suspended me from the team," he blurted at last.

"What?" Hayley gasped. She knew what a suspension could mean—not only for Stone's ego, but his future. "But why?"

"*Metro* article says I'm a druggie," he murmured. "They're testing me. Can't play till the results come back."

Hayley thought for a moment. "So—what happens when—"

"Don't," he said.

"Don't what?"

"Please. Just—don't talk right now."

Hayley took her eyes off him for the first time since she sat down.

"Hayley," he whispered. She felt his hand snake around her waist, his chin rest on her shoulder. She fought hard to keep from recoiling.

It wasn't that she didn't feel for Stone. No, that wasn't it at all. There was something else that made her want to keep her distance—something that dawned on her in a flash that very moment.

Hayley was suddenly afraid that if Stone got too close to her, he'd somehow be able to tell that his friend and teammate, Ken Davis, had driven her home from her game last week.

And if he figured that out, then maybe he'd also be able to tell how much she liked being with Ken.

Considering the situation, Hayley resolved to keep that information away from him as long as she could.

Because if he ever found out . . . it couldn't possibly end well.

JOCKS

THERE WAS A COLOSSAL sense of gloom as the crowd left the Rivington High School gym, a funereal procession of Rivington Raiders who had just been handed their first defeat of the season.

The Lady Cougars had turned the game around right after Hayley made a killer spike. They were downright giddy.

Ken ran down from his perch high atop the visitors' bleachers, taking the metal benches two at a time until he reached Hayley on the floor.

"Wow!" he cried. "Hayley, that was awesome!" Without really thinking about it, he picked her up off the floor and swung her around in a victory hug. It wasn't until she kissed him on the cheek that he realized what they were doing and abruptly set her down.

Several of the Lady Cougars gave them the eye as they walked past. One girl mumbled, only partly under her breath, "I thought she was with Stone!"

Ken waited until the rest of the team had passed before saying, "Whoa. I'm sorry, really."

"Don't worry about it," she said, brushing off the comment with a wave of her hand.

"I was just so excited for you—"

"—it's okay, really—"

"—you did such a great job tonight, you know, and—"

"Ken," Hayley cut him off. "I was wondering if you'd take me home again."

He blinked at her several times in disbelief. "You want me to . . ." He paused. "Wh-what about Coach Happy Gilmore Girls?"

"I don't think we should invite her." Hayley winked. "She probably needs to ride the bus back with the team."

Ken stared at her, moving into her eyes slowly, like sinking into quicksand. "So do you," he said, missing the joke.

"It's the last game of the regular season, Ken. She needs me for the tournament this week, so what's she going to do? Bench me *next year*? By then she'll forget all about it. Besides, for all I know, she won't even be our coach next year. So come on . . . please, I really want to drive home with you. Last time was really . . . nice."

"Last time, we were only twenty minutes away. It's like a two-hour drive back to town from Rivington." He searched her eyes. She smiled into his.

"Let's go," he said at last.

Before I lose my nerve, he added to himself.

They scurried across the parking lot and into his car.

Once they were on the road, Ken fished in his jacket pocket and fumbled around until he found his cell phone. He held it out to Hayley.

"What's that for?" she asked.

He pulled it back. "Don't you want to call Stone?"

"Why would I do that?"

"'Cause you won tonight. I mean, you guys played the hell out of Rivington—don't you think he'd want to know?"

He took the long silence that followed as a resounding *no*.

Hayley folded her arms in front of her. She stared out the window for a long time before saying, "If Stone wanted to know how we did, he could've come to the game himself." She turned to Ken. "I mean, how pathetic is that? *You* drove all the way up here to watch us play because *he* wouldn't."

Ken's heart was about to burst from embarrassment. "I came here because I wanted to," he said. "Not as your boyfriend's stand-in."

Hayley's eyes softened. "I didn't mean it like that."

They rode the next few miles in silence. Hayley was lost in thought, and Ken foolishly wished he could be inside her head. What was she thinking about? About her game-winning spike? About not riding the bus home—again? About Stone? Ken wished he knew as he struggled with a hundred things he wanted to ask her and a thousand things he wanted to say.

She beat him to it.

"Are you a virgin?" she blurted.

The question seemed to suck all the air out of his lungs. When he finally caught his breath, he answered, but it came out sounding totally lame. "No. Why?"

"Because once, in the girls' locker room, I heard Nicole tell Brittany Smith that you guys had sex. Is that true?"

Ken groaned. He glanced at Hayley, her face casting a glow in the darkness of his car. "No." He rolled his eyes. "She broke up with me before I could get anywhere with her."

"Figures," Hayley said, crossing her arms. "She said you sucked at it."

He turned his head, looked hard at her. "Did you believe her?"

She smiled. God, those dimples!

"No. I never did."

A few more miles passed in silence while the Red Hot Chili Peppers played over the radio.

"Are *you*?" Ken finally asked.

"Am I what?"

"You know . . . a virgin?"

She swung around to face him. "Is that what you're *really* asking?" she questioned, the promise of a smile hovering just behind her lips. "Or do you want to know if I've done it with Stone?"

Ken froze. "I don't know. Isn't that the same thing?"

Hayley settled back into her seat.

"We haven't," she said flatly. "Not that he hasn't tried."

There was a traffic signal just up the road. Ken slowed the car, coasting to a stop as the light changed from yellow to red.

"Can I tell you something?" she asked.

Ken nodded.

"I've always kind of liked you, you know," she whispered. "Even when we were kids, I thought you were the nicest, cutest boy in school."

He could hear something in her voice that scared him, could feel it in himself too.

"I guess what I'm trying to say is, I understand the way things are, but I wish things had turned out differently." He could see her, watching him, out of the corner of his eye, hoping to God he wasn't misreading the way she was looking at him.

Ken's heart hammered against his rib cage. He couldn't stand it anymore. He had to know if she was just playing him—or if she meant what she said.

He pulled off the side of the road, threw the car into park.

"What are you doing?" Hayley breathed.

"I know I have no right," he said, choking down his anxiety. "But . . ."

He leaned over, placed his hand gently on the back of Hayley's head. She didn't move, just stared at him with wide-open eyes.

Ken moved closer. "I *really* want to kiss you right now," he whispered.

He brought his lips softly against hers.

Hayley didn't stop him.

QUAD

EVERYONE'S EYES REMAINED FIXED on one another. A small, round wall clock ticked away seconds and then minutes as Stone continued to pound urgently on the door.

"I'm letting him in," Calvert said at last.

"Like hell!" Ranger spat. He stood square in front of him, staring him down.

Calvert wasn't backing off. "He's not the enemy—"

"He's not *your* enemy!" Ranger looked around the room. "Sage is right—he'd have no problem hurting any one of us."

Stone was still outside, alternating between pounding on the door and wrestling with the knob. "Let me in!" he urged.

Christopher tapped Ranger on the arm. "I think Calvert's right," he whispered.

Ranger narrowed his eyes at Christopher. "What the hell are you talking about!"

"Stone's scared. You can hear the panic in his voice. Just listen," Christopher insisted. He turned to face the others.

"Look, if he really wanted to hurt us, he'd just do it," he pressed. "He wouldn't sneak around."

Ranger looked over at Sage. Her eyes were red from crying. "If you open that door," she whispered, "we're all dead."

Ranger noticed Maggie in his peripheral vision. She was vehemently shaking her head.

"Maggie . . ."

"You'll be as guilty as he is," she said flatly. "You want that on your conscience?"

He turned to look at Ken, tried to gauge his position on the matter. But all Ken could do was turn away, refusing to take sides.

Ranger turned back to Christopher. "I think it's a really bad idea," he said. "Really. Bad."

Christopher's soft brown eyes met Ranger's, holding his gaze for a long, long time. "You know it's not him," he whispered. "It can't be."

"Open the door!" Stone pounded again. "*Please.*"

Ranger stared at Christopher and then at Sage. *How did this get to be my decision?* he wondered bitterly.

Let him in, Christopher mouthed.

Calvert paused for a second, maybe two, then stood up and headed for the door.

"No!" Maggie yelped as Calvert put his hands on the ice cream chest. He struggled to shove the chest out of the way. It barely budged. He shoved again. And again.

Christopher scrambled to his feet and began to shove too. After several more tries, the heavy chest was inched far enough from the door for it to partly open.

Sage tried to edge behind Ranger. She sucked in a breath as Calvert flipped the lock.

FREAKS

IT WAS HARD NOT to notice Rufus as he sailed down the H-wing hallway that afternoon on his prized long board. His hair all teased and piled chaotically on top of his head, he looked like the spawn of an unholy union between Count Dracula and the Bride of Frankenstein.

"What's with the hair, dude?" Ranger had asked at break that morning.

Rufus shrugged. "Just feeling kinda out of control today."

"Cool," Ranger had said.

But just as Rufus cruised past the end of the H building, two hundred and thirty pounds of asshole swung in front of him, blocking his safe passage off campus.

"Outta my way, stoner," Rufus said, fighting like hell to keep his voice steady.

"Or what?" Stone replied.

"Or nothing. Just move."

Stone did move. Closer to Rufus. "Or what? You'll bust me over the head with that manly skateboard?"

"I wouldn't waste the wood," Rufus countered.

It was the wrong thing to say.

Stone swooped in and pulled the long board out from under him, sending him crashing to his ass on the ground. Before Rufus could register what was happening, Stone slammed the board into the corner of the brick building, splitting it in two with a deafening *crack*.

Rufus stared at the board—the most precious possession he'd had—now split into two ragged pieces. He was too stunned to speak.

He began to lose all sense of reality. For the first time in his life he saw—actually *saw*—red. He stared at Stone—*Harold Stone, Jr.*, he reminded himself— and wanted to tear his head off with his bare hands.

Just who the fuck did *Harold* think he was? What gave him the right to screw with people the way he did?

In that moment, something about Rufus changed. Some new voice inside his head demanded justice—

demanded payment. But with Stone's goon squad backing him up, Rufus knew he didn't have a chance.

He forced himself to put the rage away, save it for another time. A time when *he* could have the upper hand.

"What the hell'd you do that for?" he demanded at last.

"I think you know," Stone said flatly.

He carefully eyed Stone's beefy features, trying to figure out if he was bluffing. He didn't want to give up the pretense, didn't want to suggest that he knew what Stone had hidden inside his PE locker that day. The suggestion was enough to drive Stone crazy for weeks.

"Let me guess—you hate my hair?" he wise-cracked instead.

"You think jokes are gonna save you?" Stone snapped, still holding the remains of what used to be the most valuable thing Rufus owned. "That was just a preview, freak. Next time, I won't knock you off the board before I break it in half."

"Bring it." Rufus's anger burbled up in him again. "I'll be waiting."

Stone threw the two pieces of wood onto the ground and closed the gap between them. Rufus could smell the testosterone seeping out of Stone's pores in the form of sweat and rage.

"Don't fuck with me, freak. Ever again. For real."

"*I* didn't fuck with *you*," Rufus screamed.

"The hell you didn't! Wrote that stupid *Metro* shit. If it wasn't you, it was one of your freak friends. Got administration all worked up, breathing down our necks . . ."

Stone looked around to make sure no one was nearby, then lowered his voice just to be sure. "If even one of us gets busted, your ass is mine, you hear me? I'll hold you personally responsible. And you know what?" He patted Rufus on the cheek, once gently, and then so sharply it stung. "Payback's a bitch!"

Rufus narrowed his eyes, raising his hand to his cheek as he watched Stone saunter off. He tried to rub away the pain as he willed the tears not to come. But they came anyway.

Hot, angry, burning tears.

You know what, Stone? he thought. *You're right. You're absolutely right.*

Payback is a bitch.

WEDNESDAY, APRIL 1

JOCKS

HAYLEY BANKS SPOTTED KEN Davis across the quad and motioned him to come over and sit with her.

"Why aren't you eating with Stone?" Ken asked.

She squinted at him for a moment. "Why aren't *you*?"

Ken shrugged. "He's kind of on a rampage today." He looked over at her to see if there was any sign of agreement from her.

Hayley didn't respond. She pulled a sandwich out of her backpack and a bottle of Gatorade. She snapped open the lid like she was wringing someone's neck.

Ken's heart gave a heavy *thump*. "Hayley?"

She began chugging and didn't stop until the Gatorade was half gone. Then she put the bottle down, replaced the cap, and turned toward Ken. "Did you know that his mom left?"

Ken's mouth pulled to one side, his cheeks filling up with embarrassment. "Doesn't everyone?"

"After all that time he spent trying to get her to stay," she said, "she just left them."

"So?" Ken asked.

Hayley pulled the sandwich out of the plastic bag but didn't bite into it. "So . . . Stone hates his dad. He never actually says it, but he does. He thinks . . . well, he thinks it's his dad's fault that his mom left. He's unhappy at home—he's unhappy pretty much anywhere lately."

Ken scrunched his face up in frustration. He knew what was going on with Stone, how hard this whole thing with his parents was. Still, he couldn't help wondering if Stone was using it justify everything else he did—to play on Hayley's sympathy—to get her to—

Hayley flicked her honey-brown hair over her shoulders. Then she turned to look at Ken. "I don't know why I started going out with him," she said, answering a question he had asked long ago. "But I can't break up with him now. Not while he's going through all of this. I'm afraid . . . I don't know. God. I'm afraid he might snap if I do."

Her eyes narrowed as she studied him, her head tilted to one side.

She laid her narrow palm on top of his. "Right now, that's all I'm saying."

Ken thought he was about to have another episode, like back in fourth grade. He turned his head away from Hayley, his face on fire.

Ken wanted to make it look like he was staring out over the quad. But in truth, he was simply hiding the smile on his face.

I can't break up with him while he's going through this, she had said.

Which meant that once it was over . . .

I'll take it, Ken thought.

That's enough. For now.

QUAD

STONE STUMBLED INTO THE student store, his eyes wild.

Ranger recoiled as Sage's nails dug into his arm.

Stone's gaze darted around the room. He was panting like a trapped animal—trying to find something to hit or throw.

Ken and Calvert tackled him. There was a confusion of bodies and a flurry of muffled movement.

It was bizarre, Ranger thought, like watching pro-wrestling on TV, only with the mute button on.

Davis and Calvert were still holding an arm apiece when Stone's chin dropped sharply to his chest. His massive shoulders began to shudder.

"Oh my God—what's wrong with him?" Maggie whispered.

Stone's knees buckled. He sank to the floor.

It took everyone a moment to realize what was happening.

"Back off!" Calvert snipped. "He's just . . . just leave him the hell alone."

Stone pushed away the hands that were holding him. The wagons circled, and everyone stood looking down at him.

He was trying not to make any noise, only he was crying too hard to do it quietly. His body heaved as he rocked back and forth on the ground. "God," he groaned through shuddering sobs. "What is going on? What the hell is going on out there?"

Ranger stared down at Harold Stone, Jr., the menace of Muir High.

He was scared—scared out of his mind the way the rest of them were.

And just that fast, it was clear. Stone wasn't the shooter.

Sage, Maggie, and Ranger alternated glances at each other. Ranger had never seen a jock cry before—didn't know it was possible.

Christopher, on the other hand, never took his eyes off Stone. Not for one second. The silence, more awkward than fearful this time, was apparently too much for him to bear. He reached out and placed his hand lightly on Stone's ropy forearm.

"It's okay," he whispered. "You're safe now. We're safe in here."

Ranger stared at Christopher and Stone and shook his head.

I hope we are *safe in here,* he thought. *Because if Stone isn't the shooter, then we still don't know who the hell is.*

DRAMA QUEENS

MR. MORGAN'S LONG WOODEN pointer was tapping madly across Europe on the pull-down map he used in class every day. Some teachers at Muir were low-tech, but Morgan was no-tech. No PowerPoint, no video, not even an overhead. Just Morgan, the pull-down map, and that dreaded pointer.

With each tap of the stick, Paisley jumped in her chair. Her nerves were shot. All week long, kids had been passing her in the hallways, singing bits of "Somewhere over the Rainbow."

A boy she barely knew approached her in English on Tuesday. "You're Paisley Reed, right?"

She'd eyed him skeptically. "Yes."

"Hey, I was wondering. Wanna go to the movies this weekend?"

The question had taken Paisley by surprise. "Well . . . I don't know. Sure, I guess."

"Great," he'd said, his grin turning into unchecked laughter. "Have a good time!" The rest of the class had burst into laughter along with him.

As if any of that wasn't bad enough, two days ago was April Fools' Day, and the pranks never seemed to end.

Copies of that awful *Metro* article had been posted on Paisley's locker door. Every time she took one down, another would go up in its place. Someone had dummied up a playbill for *Gays and Dulls*—*written by, directed by, and starring Paisley Reed*—and tucked it inside her French book. And in history, Nicole leaned so far forward in her desk, her breasts pushed into Paisley's back.

"Congratulations, I heard you made the play," she whispered.

She laughed so hard at her own joke that Mr. Morgan turned away from the chalkboard and walked down the aisle toward her. It was an unprecedented move.

"Ms. McClintock," he said. "Please take your things and sit out in the hallway for the remainder of the period."

Nicole looked stunned. She gave Paisley the evil eye on her way out. "Loser," she hissed.

So it was a little jarring when a triangle of folded paper landed on her desk during history on Friday. Sage was usually the one who sent her letters folded that way, but when Paisley looked back at her, she was busy copying the lecture notes off the board. Paisley let her eyes sweep the room. They landed on Stone. She realized with a start that he was staring at her. Her head tipped to one side, and then she saw him raise an eyebrow at her. It was just a small gesture, but it was enough for her to wonder if the note had come from him. She opened it.

Sorry about what happened to you with the drama club. There's a party tonight at Mike Massey's—everyone's gonna be there. Why don't you come?

There was no name at the bottom.

Paisley looked over at Sage to make sure she hadn't seen her with the note. Then she turned back to Stone. He was smiling at her. Her lips twitched a little as she tried to smile in return.

Maybe that's it, she thought.

Maybe she didn't fit in with the drama kids because she wasn't like the drama kids. After all, *you couldn't squeeze yourself in where you didn't belong.* She looked over at Stone again—at his perfectly straight teeth flashing in her direction.

She'd heard *he'd* had a rough time of it this week too. Suspended from the team because the

Metro had burned him—just as hard as it had burned Paisley.

Was he reaching out to her? Giving her a chance to find out where she *did* belong?

Yes. This felt right to her. Maybe this really *was* it.

Maybe Mike Massey's party could be her ticket to happiness at last.

All she had to do was fit in.

And to fit in, she needed to be more like Nicole.

Paisley knew exactly where to start.

DRAMA QUEENS

THE BIG WALK-IN PANTRY seemed more crowded than ever. *Gosh*, Paisley thought, *there's enough food in here to feed seven families for a year.* In the event of an apocalyptic disaster, Paisley was pretty sure her family would at least not die from starvation.

She'd spent the better part of the day working up the nerve to put her vague plan into motion. Now it was do or die. If she didn't act, she'd never have the chance to find out who she really was, where she really belonged.

She had to sidestep ten five-gallon bottles of water just to get to the place where her parents hid their money, inside an empty tomato can on a shelf way in the back.

The whole apocalypse preparedness thing would

have been a lot funnier if Paisley hadn't actually had to live through it. It had been this way ever since 9/11—her parents poised for disaster to strike—ready, or so they thought, because of all the crap they'd stockpiled in the pantry.

Her mom couldn't wait, it seemed, to cook in a pot over the fireplace, and her dad was ready to protect their home at a moment's notice from looters. Paisley's dad was fixated on the possibility of looters.

Paisley figured about fifty bucks would do the job. She wasn't totally sure; she'd done most of her clothes shopping at secondhand stores and so she didn't actually know how much a lemon-yellow cami, or a pair of designer jeans, or a tube of lip gloss with crushed pearls in it would cost, but she was pretty sure fifty would be enough.

Besides, it was a small enough amount that her parents would never know it was missing.

She knew exactly where to go—it would be hard not to. She sat right in the middle of those conversations between Nicole and Brittany day after day in class.

My mom took me shopping again yesterday.

My dad gave me two hundred dollars and said I could buy anything I wanted.

Paisley totally knew where those girls did their

shopping, so instead of going to science class, she slipped out to her little car, opened the newly "painted" door, and headed out to the mall.

Paisley was surprised when she got there. The mall was teeming with little old ladies with blue-washed hair. *Whoa*, she thought. *It's like this whole parallel universe—like some secret society where everyone's grandparents meet up, go to Sears, and buy polyester pants with coordinating tops.*

Paisley closed her eyes. *Grams, you never dressed like an old lady—you always had your own style.*

She smiled. Thankfully, her grams had taught her how to dress with a flair for the dramatic.

The glass doors swooshed as Paisley walked into the department store. She walked hesitantly down the aisles, looked around, tried to orient herself. She rarely went to the mall, and she *never* went to upscale stores like this one. There had never been a reason to—until now.

Paisley's heart quickened as she spotted something in her peripheral vision. She craned her neck, strained to see around a carousel of poly-blend gauchos. Though it was most of the way across the store, she could easily read the sign above it: Juniors. And directly below the sign . . . camis. Racks and racks of them. Lemon yellow, hot pink, ice blue. An otherworldly glow haloed the rack as Paisley made her way toward it. She pulled a cami off the hanger.

Mint julep green, with pearly buttons down the front.

She held it against herself, pressed it to her chest, and spun giddy circles in the aisle. In a nearby mirror, she caught a glimpse of green as she twirled. She moved forward and stood before the mirror, holding up the shimmery cami to see how she would look with it on. She smiled at her reflection.

No, I have to see how it really looks, Paisley thought with a renewed sense of urgency.

A salesclerk pointed her to the try-on rooms, and Paisley practically danced her way into the cubicle. *After this,* she thought, *I'll find a cute pair of jeans. Oh! And then, cosmetics.*

The silky material was cool against her skin as the cami slithered over her head, then her breasts. She had never worn a shirt without a bra before. It felt daring. She fingered the cute little buttons that sparingly held the front together. Paisley was sure she looked beautiful, but she had her back to the mirror.

Somehow, she was nervous about seeing herself. If the cami looked the way it felt, it really could be her moment to shine—the new and improved

Paisley Reed, no longer a drama-queen wannabe but a girl who could hold her own with the quad elite.

She turned finally, sucked in a breath.

Oh my God.

I look just like Nicole McClintock.

It was the closest thing to a makeover that Paisley could ever have imagined. One last shot at a debut: not as some mediocre actress, like the *Metro* article had said, but at being pretty. At being accepted.

She hurried out of the cami and back into her old clothes. As she passed the counter, she asked the salesclerk, "Can you tell me where the jeans are?"

"Third floor," the saleswoman said. "But you'll have to pay for the shirt before you go up there." She must have noticed the surprise on Paisley's face because she added, "I'm sorry . . . store policy."

"Oh," Paisley said. "Okay." She laid the cami on the counter as if it were made of hummingbird eggs.

The woman ran her scanner over the price tag and hit a couple of buttons on the cash register. "That will be eighty-six forty-nine."

"Eighty-six!" Paisley's mouth dropped open. "Dollars?"

"That's actually the sales price. It's regularly a hundred."

"*Dollars?*" Paisley said again, thinking about the

single bill in her bag. She wouldn't have enough for the other things she wanted to get. She didn't even have enough for the cami.

"I . . . I don't . . . I only have fifty," she finally managed.

The saleswoman looked empathetic. "I can put it on layaway. Maybe you can save your allowance."

Paisley knew the suggestion was well meant, but it didn't help.

"I can't," she said, near tears. "I mean . . . I don't have time. *I need it tonight.*"

The saleswoman shrugged apologetically.

It was the final defeat.

Paisley glanced up at the woman, unable to keep the tears out of her eyes. "I'll just put this back," she whispered.

At home, she found the makeshift tomato can/bank and put the fifty-dollar bill back inside. Then she fingered the soft mint green material inside the main compartment of her denim sack.

Her parents would never know.

And neither would the lady at the department store.

QUAD

"WELL, IF IT'S NOT Stone," Sage whispered, "then who is it?"

Calvert shrugged. "I'm telling you, it's gotta be Rufus Dockins. Have you seen him the last few days? Something has seriously gone *snap*."

Ranger's breath caught in his throat. Rufus? Could he do something like this?

As incredible as the notion seemed, Calvert was right. Something *had* changed with Rufus over the past few days. Maybe weeks. Something inside him had grown darker.

Ranger had seen it himself the night of Massey's party.

"You think it's Rufus?" Maggie scoffed. "Try one of your juicer buddies. You've heard of 'roid rage, haven't you? You guys load up on that shit all the time."

"Just like you loaded up on something at Massey's party." Sage's words drifted toward Stone. "Isn't that right?"

"I don't know what you're talking about," Stone mumbled, dropping his head onto his hands. He seemed to blanch at the very mention of Massey's name.

"You bastard," Maggie whispered to herself, but in the closeness of the room, every sound was magnified. Heads swung in her direction. "You guys are such hypocrites. You go around accusing everyone else of being freaks and losers when you're the biggest loser on the planet. You don't even have the balls to cheat on your girlfriend like a man. You have to go after some helpless girl at a—"

"You don't know what the hell you're talking about," Calvert grated. "You weren't at that party."

Ranger shuddered as Maggie drilled into Stone with her eyes. "You think everything you do is under the radar, don't you? That you can get away with anything just because you can run thirty yards with a ball tucked under your arm. Well, you're not under the radar, Stone. Not anymore." A crazed grin flickered across her face. "There are eyes everywhere."

"What do you mean, *eyes everywhere?*" Ken shifted his gaze from Maggie to Stone. "What the hell is she talking about?"

But Stone didn't respond. He just sat there, struggling to keep his face steady.

"Oh my God," Ranger gasped.

Everyone seemed to have forgotten about him as he'd slipped into silence. He'd been searching his mind for clues, offhanded comments, wayward hints that Rufus might have hit the wall the other night with all his destruction talk.

Ranger turned to Maggie, but his eyes passed right through her.

Theo, he said inside his head.

Theo Martin . . .

"Theo was making an underground video," Ranger blurted.

A couple of people gasped, "What?"

Maggie glared at Ranger. Shook her head in disgust. "How could you?"

"I'm sorry," he rushed. A long, throbbing pause followed. He was waiting for Maggie to fill in the rest, to give Theo up as the shooter, but she didn't. She just sat there, burning holes in him with her eyes.

"Maggie," he finally prodded, "we're trapped on the floor of the student center while someone outside is shooting a gun."

"Uh, yeah. I noticed," she said, her words heavy with sarcasm.

"You have to tell us. Do you know anything about it?"

"Why would I know anything?" Maggie countered. A little too defensive, maybe?

Ranger narrowed his eyes at her. "Where's Theo?"

Maggie tugged at the oversized T-shirt she was wearing without answering.

"Maggie," Ranger pressed. "*Where is he?*"

"How should I know?" She seemed annoyed.

"Look," he said, "I know all about the video. I know he was at Massey's party that night. He caught Stone on tape with that girl—"

Stone looked suddenly panicked. "Hey!" he yelped as Calvert hissed at Ranger, "Screw you!"

Ranger ignored them and continued. "He got it all on film. *Everything,*" he added with dramatic emphasis.

He wanted to push Maggie's buttons. Wanted her to tell him something. Anything.

But Maggie just crossed her arms and turned her head away.

She wasn't talking.

TECHIES

"WELL?" MAGGIE GRINNED, WAVING a copy of the now-infamous *Metro* at Theo. She giggled, then tacked the paper to her corkboard. "What do you think?"

Theo put his hand on the back of her head and kissed her, hard, without answering. He noticed Maggie's face darken as she backed away from him.

"No, seriously," she said. "What did you think about it?"

Theo wiped saliva off his bottom lip. "It was definitely the most controversial issue yet."

Her face clouded over. "You hated it," she whispered.

"No, I didn't." Theo closed the tenuous gap between them. "I thought it was awesome. It's all I've heard about this week. That's the mark of great journalism, right?"

She turned her head, looked at him, drove her eyes deep into his. It killed him when she looked at him that way. There was nowhere to hide from her.

"Tell me the truth," she said flatly.

He shrugged. "Okay, look. Some of the articles were a little harsh. Like the one about the play. 'Cause, I mean, I like Paisley. She's harmless, you know? She never hurt anyone."

Maggie slitted her eyes at Theo.

"But overall, it was an awesome paper." He reached out to her as if he were touching a priceless artifact: gently—with great respect and just a little fear. He turned her around. "Maggie, it was awesome. Magnolia. My Magnolia. You got the school talking—isn't that what you wanted?"

She shrugged. "I guess."

Theo pulled her toward the bed. He hated how far away she felt, even though she was standing right there. "Aren't you proud of yourself?" he asked.

"Yeah."

He tugged at her, pulling her closer. "*I'm* proud of you."

That got her smiling.

"How proud?" she asked, uncharacteristically flirty.

"*Very* proud."

They kissed for what seemed like hours. Then Maggie held a hand against his chest.

"My mom's working graveyard tonight."

Theo sprang to attention at the news.

"Can you stay?" she asked.

He nodded enthusiastically.

But Maggie's hand pressed harder against his rib cage. "Theo?"

"Yeah?" he panted, trying to kiss her neck.

Maggie propped herself on her elbows. "I keep thinking about what you told me."

"What'd I tell you?" he mumbled into her hair.

"About Stone and Nicole and your SAT scores. Your scholarship."

The words landed on Maggie's bed with a nearly audible thud. He reluctantly unwound himself from her.

"Why are you thinking about *that*?" he asked.

"Because I want to finish what we started."

He frowned. "Let me rephrase—why are you thinking about that *now*?"

Maggie ignored the question. "Are you committed to going through with the plan?" she asked.

Theo panicked for a moment. *Which plan? The plan for me to stay over tonight? Or the plan to—*

"Theo?"

He blinked against his confusion, but there was nothing confusing about the look in Maggie's eyes.

"Yes," he said. "Absolutely."

He could see her shoulders visibly relax. "Good," she said. "Because Mike Massey's having a party tonight."

Theo shrugged. "So?"

"So I think you could finish what we started if you went over there."

He searched Maggie's face. She was right, of course. That party would be the perfect opportunity for him to take care of business. Everyone who owed him would be there. At the same time, he had to weigh that opportunity against what he might miss if he left her home, alone.

"Maybe there's a better time to do this," he suggested.

"Don't worry. When you're done, come back here so we can . . . you know. Celebrate."

Maggie leaned over and kissed Theo's lips, which were pursed in thought.

"This may not be the best way to persuade me to go," he mumbled against her mouth.

Maggie leaned back and studied Theo through narrowed eyes. "You're not going there just because you got screwed out of a scholarship," she reminded him. "You're going because of what they did to *me*. Because of what they do to everyone. Every day." Her head tilted to one side. "Don't lose sight of the goal, Theo."

Theo's eyes stung. She was right. It had to be tonight.

"So you promise that when I get back—"

"When you get back," she said with a smile, "I'll be your Magnolia. For real."

Theo took a long, deep breath.

"Pinkie swear," he said.

CHOIRBOYS

Perry sat up on his bed. A quick glance at the alarm clock told him he'd missed dinnertime by several hours. It didn't matter; he wasn't hungry. He surveyed his bed, which was littered with wadded-up tissue.

God, he was such a snot factory when he cried, and it seemed like he'd been crying all week. He shook his head and pulled another Kleenex out of the box.

I knew Christopher wasn't over Stone, he thought. *He said he was, but he's not.*

Maybe it wouldn't have mattered so much if Perry hadn't taken the hit for Christopher's indiscretion. But he did, and it still hurt.

Stone was out there, walking around like it was

nothing. And Christopher still couldn't see what his stupid, unreachable dream was doing to Perry.

It was tearing his insides to shreds.

After the Pommes Frites incident, Christopher had promised that he'd prove his loyalty to Perry, that he'd make things right again between them. It was clear by now that none of those things were going to happen. And if Perry ever hoped to see an end to the agony he suffered at the hands of people like Stone, it was obvious he'd have to do it himself.

Perry moved to his closet, dug around in the back for the shoe box he swore he'd never lay his hands on. He'd buried the weapon back there moments after his father had given it to him. Some vain effort to spur manly interests in him, Perry supposed. Protect and serve—what a joke.

Good job, Dad, he thought. *I'm interested now. I bet you'd be proud.*

He shoved the cold metal object into his jeans pocket, where it made a noticeable bulge. He slipped on a jacket. Tried it there. Yeah, it fit much better in his outside pocket anyway.

As he went into the bathroom, he peeked around the corner, saw that his mom was in her room watching TV. Fine with him; it would make it easier to slip out the front door. He zipped his fly and went to wash his hands in the sink. That's when he made the mistake of looking up and catching a glimpse of his face in the mirror.

The scab on his nose had already fallen off, leaving behind a deep red welt. Until that moment, he'd managed to avoid looking directly at the cut he'd gotten at Pommes Frites that day. But he was so preoccupied by with what he was about to do that he'd caught himself off guard.

As he studied the scar, he knew intellectually that it would lighten over time. But still, it would always be there: an unmistakable, permanent reminder of being hated. The wounds that he'd been able to carry hidden and invisible for fifteen years were now front and center, for the entire world to see. Including himself, every time he looked in a mirror.

It was a wrong he couldn't let go un-righted.

He felt around inside the pocket of his jacket. Yes, it was still there.

After another quick peek down the hall to verify that his mother was distracted, Perry was clear to leave the apartment unnoticed.

FRIDAY, APRIL 3

PREPS

NICOLE SHOWED UP AT Brittany's house around seven to help her get ready for the party and to formulate a plan.

"Make sure you have a couple of beers," Nicole advised as she ran the flat iron through Brittany's newly highlighted hair. Brittany had had a dramatic tantrum earlier that week. Her skanktastic mom had been going out a lot lately, leaving Brit to help out with her little brother way too much. So when she threw down the I-took-care-of-his-stupid-teacher-for-you gauntlet, Brittany's mom took her to get her hair colored and her nails done. It was the easiest way to shut her up.

"But don't drink too much," Nicole continued. "You don't want to pass out or, even worse, puke before you can finish what you started. If you know what I mean." She punctuated the advice with a lingering giggle.

"Okay, drink a little, but not too much," Brittany repeated as if she were taking mental notes.

"And remember what it says in *Cosmo Girl*: spruce to seduce."

"No, it doesn't."

"Yes, it does, Brittany. In 'Put the Crush on Your Crush.' God! Don't you ever *read*?"

"I must've missed that issue."

"Okay. So we need to pick out a hot outfit, one that screams 'Take me off!' Are you getting all this?" Nicole demanded.

"Yes, Nicole. Shit! Don't talk to me like I'm a five-year-old."

"Okay, well, you're kind of being a 'tard right now. I just wanted to make sure."

"I get it. I'm totally listening to you."

Nicole ran another lock of Brittany's hair through the flat iron. "So what are you going to say to him?"

Brittany's eyes fluttered upward. "What do you mean?"

Nicole clicked her tongue in exasperation. "Well, you can't just go up to him and be all, *Doi*! You have to say something profound."

"How about, *Here's your Ritalin?*"

"Oh my God, please tell me you're not going to be that much of a nerd."

"What do you mean?"

"Try to be more, like, subtle."

"Like what?"

"Like, *I'm gonna go get something to wash this down—care to join me?*"

"You think *I* should take some Ritalin?"

"Huh? No, Brittany. No. The Ritalin's for Stone!"

"I don't get it." Brittany pouted. "Why are you saying I should—"

Nicole slammed the flat iron onto the bathroom counter. "You need to have something to say to him, okay? Go into the bathroom with him, give him the Ritalin, and then invite him into *another* room. Show him what he's missing by going out with that closet dyke, if you get what I'm saying. Let him know what it's like to be with a real woman."

Nicole's eyes glistened as she picked up the iron again. "This party can be the beginning of everything, Brittany. I mean, you've been waiting for tonight for such a long time. Aren't you ready for a changing day in your life?"

Brittany frowned. "Wait a minute . . . isn't that from the beginning of the *Dr. Phil Show?*"

Nicole's cheeks pinked slightly. Damn it. Had she actually absorbed something from one of her mother's pathetic TV shows?

She clucked her tongue and moved on. "You're missing the point," she said. "This will be an evening to remember if you just do what I tell you. Okay?"

Brittany, who had been watching Nicole in the mirror as she spoke, let her gaze drift to her own reflection. For a moment she looked disoriented, as if she were surprised to see herself there.

"Omigod!" she squealed without warning. "I look totally cute!"

FRIDAY, APRIL 3

FREAKS

RUFUS PICKED UP ON the third ring.

"What do you wanna do tonight?" Ranger asked.

"I dunno, dude. You?"

Ranger shrugged, not thinking about the fact that Rufus couldn't see him. "Too bad we already smoked all that bud."

"Yeah."

Ranger was up in his room, picking out a made-up song on a bass guitar that wasn't plugged in. *I should really learn how to play this thing*, he thought. He'd wanted to take guitar that year, but he couldn't fit the elective into his current schedule, which was cramped with requirements. "Wanna come over and play Halo 2?"

"I dunno. I'm kinda bored with that," Rufus mumbled. "It's not real life, you know?"

"What's going on, dude? I haven't seen you in a couple of days, and now you sound all emo," Ranger said.

"Friggin' Stone busted my long board after school Wednesday."

"Why the hell'd he do that?"

"He thinks we wrote those *Metro* articles."

Ranger tuned the E string on his bass. "He thinks we wrote the *Metro*? That's funny. The two most unmotivated guys in school."

"It's *not* funny," Rufus snapped. "Jesus, Ng—one way or another, that crazy bastard is gonna kick our asses. Don't you get that?"

"Okay, okay, jeez. Why didn't you just tell him it wasn't us?"

"I tried," Rufus said. "I don't think he believed me."

"Well, I mean, the guy's a Neanderthal, but he's not a total idiot. He'll figure it out."

Rufus responded as if he hadn't heard Ranger at all. "I wish the dude would just, like . . . disappear. Know what I mean? Like I want us to go to school on Monday and have him just be . . . gone."

He paused. "A school without Stone," he added wistfully. "What would that be like?"

"Pretty sweet," Ranger agreed.

"Yeah, well," Rufus grumbled. "Somebody should make it happen."

They let the line buzz between them for a while as Ranger picked away at his bass. He wished he could figure out how to play it for once and for all. He'd been scratching on that thing since he was in sixth grade.

"We could go downtown and get a Slurpee or something," Rufus said.

Ranger thought about it as he played a mad riff that sounded much better without sound than it would have amplified. "I could use a little caffeine, I guess. How 'bout I meet you on the corner in five?"

* * *

They were sitting on the curb in front of the 7-Eleven, Ranger sipping a Mountain Dew Big Gulp and Rufus working his way through a full-sized bag of Funyuns.

That was when the parade started.

First they saw one solitary jock drive by in a sports car.

Then that tall skinny dude passed by, the one with the zits. One of the basketball players, maybe?

Ranger narrowed his eyes.

They all look alike, he thought.

A few minutes later those two ditzy cheerleaders sped by, their hair blowing out the car window like victory banners.

Then a car load of basketball demigods pulled into the parking lot and screeched to a stop, inches from where Rufus's and Ranger's feet sat perched on their skateboards. The jocks cut the engine, and the heavy bass, which could be heard all the way down the street, died along with it. Jock laughter bounced into the parking lot as the boys pushed their way into the store.

"Let Brophy do it," one of them said. "He's got the ID."

"And the sprouts to back it up," someone added as they dribbled a round of hoots and hollers between them.

"Hey, and get some Trojans while you're at it," someone else called out. "I heard Nicole McClintock's gonna be there!"

Peals of laughter swarmed around Rufus and Ranger, who turned away from the circus inside the store and flicked their eyes at each other.

"Jerk-offs," Ranger said.

Rufus popped a Funyun in his mouth and then pointed across the street. "Hey—there goes Theo Martin."

Theo was across the street, in front of the Starbucks. Neither of them bothered to call over because there was no way he'd hear them through all the traffic on Front Street. They watched as he slipped something into his shirt pocket—looked kind of like a pack of cigs from a distance—then hop on his bike and speed off in the same direction as the rest of the jock parade.

"You think he's . . . ?" Ranger started to say.

"Nah." Rufus shook his head. "Why would he have anything to do with a juicer party?"

The pack of jocks jumped back into their car and amped up the bass until Rufus and Ranger were practically bouncing off the curb. They pulled away, drunk with glee and soon-to-be vodka.

"Still," Rufus added. "Theo, heading off in the same direction? It *is* kind of weird."

"Yeah." Ranger blew into the extra-long straw sticking out of his Slurpee. "Man, I wish we still had some of that bud. I need to come down off this caffeine a little."

"Why don't we put that caffeine to good use?" Rufus suggested. He stood up on his deck, pushed off with his left foot.

"I'm feeling like a little trouble. Come on. Let's go find out what Martin is up to."

JOCKS

STONE FELT LIKE HE'D been waiting for this party for weeks.

Mike Massey's parents were classic for taking off, and not just out of town, like Hayley's parents sometimes did. Massey's folks would jet to places like Aruba for a long weekend, leaving their bonehead son alone in that amazing house of theirs, trusting him to "mind the store." The monolithic two-story structure was designed by Massey's architect dad, furnished by his interior decorator mom, and was once featured in *No One Needs a House This Big Monthly*. It boasted six bedrooms (more than enough for the three people who lived there), an in-home gym, an in-home theater, and a rec room. The backyard had a fully stocked wet bar and a swimming pool/Jacuzzi that were the cornerstones of many of his "minding the store" parties. The extra bedrooms were perfect for party-night hookups: since Massey's folks had daily maid service, he just threw the sheets on the floor and the maid put it all back together before his parents returned from their exotic ports of call.

Man, that house had everything. Everything Stone's place didn't have. Not anymore.

Brad Calvert, Stone, and a couple of the others were wheeling out the second of two kegs by the time the basketball team showed up. Dozens of people were already hanging out in that multi-million-dollar house, drinking beer and dancing to the music that was pounding out of Massey's insane home-theater system, and more were pouring in every few minutes.

An explosion of frenzied cheering carried into the house from the back deck. Ted Hooks, the captain of the basketball team, had finally arrived. *The* Eagle *has landed.*

"That was a freaking awesome game!" Brad Calvert screamed against the noise.

"No, dude, you missed the best part," Hooks told him. "Twain's guard shoots from outside the key with like two seconds left and sinks it! So now, Twain's up by one, but the ref calls a foul on their center, who's trying to block Washington. Washington"—Hooks struck a pose, poised to shoot an imaginary ball— "goes up . . . releases . . . it's good!"

Another cheer burst into the sky like fireworks. Plastic beer tumblers lifted together in some kind of inarticulate, slurred chant that sounded a little like, "Mark Twain ducks ticks," by those still sober enough to understand it.

Stone said a silent prayer of thanks that he was not one of those people. He chugged the rest of his beer and then elbowed Calvert. "Where the hell is Davis? I thought he was gonna be here tonight."

Calvert raised his eyebrows at Stone before sputtering a bit of nervous laughter. "How should I know?" He took another stab at laughing, but it still didn't come out right.

"Hold on." Stone narrowed his eyes at Calvert. "I don't believe you. Where is he?"

"I don't know, man, I'm telling you." Calvert cleared his throat.

Stone felt every ounce of good humor drain from his body.

Calvert caved. "Okay, look, I don't know this for sure, but Kendra Marsh is on the Lady Cougars and she told me that Davis was at their last game, the one against Lewis and Clark."

Stone's forehead wrinkled. "Why would Davis be at a . . ."

Wait a minute. Ken had practically chewed Stone out for not going to any of Hayley's volleyball games. Could that little punk be . . . ?

"Was he with Hayley?" Stone asked. He hoped Calvert hadn't heard the slight catch in his voice.

"Dude, seriously, I don't know anything. I told you everything I heard."

Stone stared at his empty beer cup as Calvert stumbled off. His jaw throbbed as he sat there, blinking back tears.

Hayley? *And Davis?*

Stone didn't know what to do with that.

And then, he almost laughed.

He didn't know what to do—Jesus Christ, just like his old man.

"Hey!" he barked at the next person who walked by. He stuck his empty beer cup in the kid's hand. "Get me another one. *Now!*"

TECHIES

THEO DIDN'T HAVE MUCH time to figure out the best way to hide his camera. Obviously the pants-pocket technique wouldn't work. As Rufus and Ranger had pointed out at lunch the other day, the recording light was visible through the mesh. Not only that, but he wouldn't have very good control of the angle. And he couldn't just keep the camera hidden in his waistband like he did during that math test.

So where?

His shirt pocket would probably offer the closest thing to a bird's-eye view without pointing a lens directly at his subjects; plus, it would be pretty easy to control. Minor technicality: How would he be able to actually videotape through the fabric of his shirt?

Theo's mind operated with computerlike speed.

He pulled out his pocketknife and scraped a hole in his shirt pocket. It didn't look at all out of place—blended right in with the vast array of holes in both his shirts. He was planning on just dropping the camera inside until he spotted an empty cigarette pack in a trash can. He slid the camera into the package, marked where the lens hit, then used his knife again to carve out a peephole. It was a great plan. Now if anyone were to ask what was in his pocket, he could just say, *Pack o' smokes*, and it wouldn't be a complete lie.

His body still ached with unwanted separation from Maggie. But his mind played and replayed her words as he hopped back on his bike and continued his way to Hyde Glen Park, the upscale neighborhood where Mike Massey lived.

I keep thinking about what you told me.

About Stone and Nicole and your SAT scores.

You're going because of what they did to me.

Because of what they do to everyone.

The words pumped in his veins, pushing him forward.

He didn't have to wonder which house was Massey's—it was a zoo by the time he got there. Theo couldn't even guess how many people were there; mobs of people hung out inside and spilled off the back deck, too. There were so many people at that party, Theo thought, he was almost positive no one would notice him. In fact, he probably could have walked around with his camera in plain view and not attracted undue attention as he filmed.

But that wasn't Theo's mission tonight. This job had to be done on the down-low.

He tried to make his way to the living room, but it took him nearly five minutes just to get through the entry hall. A girl he knew from his English class was standing right next to his armpit, and as she turned sharply away from him, some of her beer sloshed onto his shoe. *Great . . . nothing like the stench of stale beer. That'll be a huge turn-on for Maggie when I get back.* His body burned at the sound of her name in his head. He wished he were kissing her just then instead of prying his way through a flock of drunken, horny kids he hated. *I'm doing this for her*, he reminded himself, *all for my Magnolia.* She'd done her part by slitting the proverbial throat of Muir High, and now he had to keep up his end by decapitating the beast.

The footage he got as he entered Massey's house was pretty good stuff, showcasing the lack of restraint typical in that kind of house party.

He got it all: the booze, the kegs, the pills, and the

pot—the brightest lights of the school doing all of the above. Parents, teachers, everyone would be shocked when they saw the truth. But Theo had a grander mission. He needed to find Stone and the steroid posse, all the preps and jocks that seemed to move through the world encased in some kind of protective force field.

They got ahead by tearing others down. By plotting and cheating. Taking credit for grades they hadn't earned while people like Theo and Maggie never seemed to catch a break. That was the way those jocks' and preps' world seemed to rotate. They didn't care who they destroyed in the process.

He had to show everyone that they weren't worthy of the attention they commanded—of the breath they drew.

A thunderclap of commotion ripped Theo back into the here and now. He spun around in time to see Nicole McClintock and Brittany Smith making their grand entrance, riding laughter into the room like it was Cinderella's carriage. Without even having to ask, they each had a beer in their hand, and they quickly became the nucleus of activity in the cavernous living room.

As if by magic, a path opened before them, allowing them to move anywhere without getting caught up like Theo had. Throngs of devotees and hopefuls followed them wherever they went. Silent, secret bets were made regarding which of the two girls would end up with which top-level jock in one of the extra bedrooms that night. It was anyone's guess at a party like this.

Theo locked his sights on Nicole and Brittany while making every effort to keep himself out of everyone else's way.

Soon, he knew, they'd give him all the justification he needed to follow through.

To finish, as Maggie said, what had already been started.

CHOIRBOYS

HE KNEW WHOSE HOUSE the party was at. Of course he knew. It was all anyone had talked about that week. It wasn't hard to figure out where Mike Massey lived, either. In fact, it was child's play.

While the mostly empty city bus bumped along, Perry kept feeling the outside of his jacket pocket, reassured by the knowledge that, like the jocks, now he too had backup.

He walked up to Mike Massey's house and found two huge football players stationed at the door.

Gargoyles, Perry thought.

His throat constricted as he approached the door. He pretended that he didn't see the monsters and intended to walk right into the house.

The plan was short-lived. One of them stuck his huge paw against Perry's bony chest.

"Who invited you?" the gargoyle asked.

The unexpected interrogation threw Perry completely off script. He scrambled for an answer. "Uh . . . Stone," he croaked, swallowing against the dryness of his throat.

"I don't think so, slim."

"But I'm just going in to—"

"Beat it," the other gargoyle cut in.

Perry's glance shifted between them for a few seconds. "Can't I just—"

The first gargoyle leaned over, breathing rancid air right in Perry's face. "Get the hell outta here."

Perry stared into the monster's eyes—shivered as beads of sweat formed on his forehead. He found the heavy object in his pocket, gripped the handle.

He willed himself to show it, to put the gargoyle in its place, but his hand wouldn't obey.

He hadn't seen this coming. He thought he'd be able to just waltz inside, go find Stone, and—

Perry backed down the driveway, fumbling as he bumped into one of the many cars parked there. The gargoyles on the step laughed. As soon as he reached the street, he bolted.

He was out of breath by the time he got to the bus stop, which was pretty far away from Massey's house.

On the ride home, Perry pounded his fists on his

thighs. He leaned back and banged his head against the window until he noticed the bus driver watching him in the rearview mirror. His face contorted as he fought off a fresh wave of tears.

Perry shoved his hands in his pockets and felt the cold metal against his fingertips. Christ, why hadn't he used it? He could have at least tried. Instead, all he did was prove to them that everything they'd ever said about him was true. And more.

Not the next time, Perry thought, squaring his jaw. *Next time I will not back down.*

JOCKS

STONE PUT HIS NOSE in the air and sniffed. Where the hell were Nicole and Brittany? Since Hayley wasn't showing up, he had no reason not to get his hands on that Ritalin they'd promised.

Who am I kidding? Stone told himself. *If what Calvert said was even a little bit true, then I'm being played—big time.*

A little Ritalin would help ease the sting.

"Yo, man!" Stone slurred as Calvert carried four or five tumblers of beer onto the back deck. "You seen Nicole?"

"In there." Calvert smiled, jabbing his elbow toward the house. "With Brittany. You can't hardly miss 'em."

Stone broke out in a smile. He'd been itching to catch a buzz all day. It wasn't far from his mind, either, that he might score a little Nicole too. That would serve Ken Davis right. Bagging the chick that had dumped him. It would serve Hayley right too. Stone knew how much his girlfriend—ex-girlfriend—hated pretty much everyone on the cheer squad.

As he staggered his way toward the living room, Hayley's face swam before him. God, he'd wasted so much time on that bitch. Every time he'd tried to make his move, there was always another story. *I can't tonight—I have practice. We're getting together Saturday at Kendra's for a team party. This Friday? No, we've got an away game. You could come, you know.*

Yeah, right. Like he'd ever drive out to Biggs, or East Biggs, or East freaking Nicholas to watch her team get creamed by a bunch of hairy she-men. That was his dad's game. Chase some skirt around, begging for a little play. A little attention. But not him.

Except, for some reason, when it came to Hayley.

If I go to your stupid away game, will you make it worth my while? he'd ask. And she'd answer with that smile, those dimples, that soft laugh that reeled him in at first but lately was nothing more than a big fat freaking NO dressed in volleyball shorts.

Christ, could it really be adding up to that? And after all that time with Hayley and nothing to show for it, Ken Davis started making an appearance at her games?

Stone shook his head. *What the hell am I waiting for?* Why was it so hard to just cut his losses?

The truth was, he usually got laid before having to move on. Maybe that was why he was having so much trouble letting go. To the victor go the spoils, but he hadn't yet won his prize.

I'm ready to get what I want, he thought. *Only Hayley isn't here to give it to me. Shit!*

His gaze ricocheted around the cavernous house. He was on overdrive. He needed that goddamn Ritalin. He needed Nicole. Anything to dull the noise in his head. Because if he couldn't make sense out of what was going on with Hayley, then he needed everything to stop making sense.

Stone banged his fist against the wall behind him. Shook the dust out of his head.

Screw this, he decided at last. *Harold Stone the First begs for play—and I'm not Harold!!!*

"Stone!"

He assumed it was Nicole McClintock calling his name. *Finally!* he thought. *Let's get this party started!*

He swung around. . . .

DRAMA QUEENS

SAGE SAW PAISLEY NEARLY every day after school. Sometimes they'd even ride home together. But Paisley's car wasn't parked in its usual spot at three o'clock, and Sage had begun to wonder.

At first it was a vague question in her mind: *Where could Paisley be?* But after a while, the vagueness turned to worry, and before too long, the worry turned to fear.

Sage knew Paisley wasn't thinking clearly. Starting with the auditions and ending with that awful article in the *Metro*, it had been a hellish week for her. And the teasing hadn't stopped yet.

Sage began wonder—had someone taken a prank against Paisley too far? Or worse, with Paisley's fragile psyche, could she be thinking about hurting herself?

After trying to call Paisley a dozen times or more, Sage finally went over to her house.

Paisley's little Honda with the silver-wrapper door wasn't parked out front where it normally would have been. She could knock, but she didn't want to freak out Paisley's folks, who were already a little on the wound-up side.

"Paranoid conspiracy theorists," Paisley sometimes called them. They'd have search and rescue and Channel 13 News on their front lawn in less than fifteen minutes if Sage even hinted she didn't know where Paisley was.

So, where are you? Sage wondered again. Her breath grew shallow as she fought off the encroaching fear with every ounce of restraint she could muster. It was like living a scene out of some awful teen slasher flick, where the camera sits fixed on the heroine's horrified face while the background spins sickeningly behind her.

She camped out on Paisley's porch, but as the minutes ticked by, there was still no trace of Paisley. *Where could she be?*

Sage decided to take a walk to the local 7-Eleven. It was a long shot, she knew, but it would at least keep her from freaking out entirely. She was standing just off the corner of a busy intersection when a car came whizzing by; she found herself leaping backward onto the sidewalk to avoid getting hit. She came this close to shouting profanity at the driver until she noticed who the driver was.

It was Nicole McClintock, and Brittany Smith was with her. They were heading to a Friday-night party. Sage was almost certain of it.

She watched Nicole's car until it disappeared around a corner, trailing behind it a ribbon of random images: the audition, the *Metro* article, Paisley's withdrawal after the article came out.

Sage knew how badly Paisley wanted to be part of something. To belong somewhere. All she wanted was to be like Nicole, universally accepted and loved.

So, what would be next on her list? Sage wondered. *Where would Paisley try to fit in now?*

Sage tried to think of who she could call, who might know something, *anything*, about Paisley. The only person she could think of was Christopher Jakes. He and Paisley weren't friends exactly, but she and Christopher had spent time at the same health club last summer—sitting on beach chairs and engaging in what Christopher called "Boy Scouting."

Christopher wasn't mean to her, like the others. Maybe he *could* help.

Sage called information to get his number. When he picked up, she got right down to business. "I'm looking for Paisley. You wouldn't happen to know where she is, would you?"

"Why would *I* know where Paisley is?" Christopher asked on the other end of the line.

"I'm not sure," Sage mumbled, feeling stupid all of a sudden. "I just figured . . . I'm kind of worried about her, that's all. How's your eye, by the way?"

"It's healing." She could hear Christopher sigh on the other end of the line. "Okay, listen, I heard something in choir the other day," he said finally.

"What was it?"

"Calvert and those guys were talking about a prank Nicole was planning. Something about a party, maybe? I wasn't really listening, but I thought I heard them mention Paisley's name—and something about payback for getting Nicole into trouble."

Sage closed her eyes. Oh God. It was as bad as she'd feared.

"I'm glad Paisley's moving into the twenty-first century, though," Christopher added. "That might help."

Sage's eyebrows folded together. "What do you mean?"

"I saw her come out of the bathroom at Taco Bell after school today. She had the cutest little green cami on, with these beautiful buttons down the front. She looked fabulous. And who knew she had such a rack? In fact, when I first saw her, I almost thought she was Nicole McClintock."

The hair on Sage's neck stood on end. She flashed to the conversation she'd overheard in Señor Frog's class one day.

Where's the party? Nicole had asked Stone.

There's one at Massey's, but not till after April Fools'.

Sage had no idea where Mike Massey lived. She had never been to one of *those* parties.

And neither had Paisley. She'd be like a lamb to the slaughter.

Sage thanked Christopher and quickly hung up. She dialed information and got an address for Massey in Hyde Glen Park. Nicole and Brittany had been headed in that direction. That had to be it.

QUAD

SILENCE BLISTERED THE AIR inside the student store.

Ranger was having trouble catching his breath. He thought about the sign hanging out front, CAPACITY—30, and realized that a lot more people could have fit in there with them. Even so, he felt like they were all stacked on top of each other, sardine style. He had to fight the impulse to rebel against the relative quiet by screaming at the top of his lungs.

Moments of silence ticked by slower than they should have, it seemed, as the labored breathing of fear and panic filled the small room. The air hung thick with the sickening smell of melting candy, and Ranger wondered if he was the only one who felt like he wanted to puke.

Maggie had turned away from Ranger, but he continued to stare at her anyway. "So you don't know where Theo is?" he asked again.

The far-off sound of two-way radios began drifting toward the student store, and soon after, Ranger became aware of muted footsteps all around them. But he couldn't tell what direction they were coming from. How far away they were, or who they belonged to.

Yet through it all, the only thing Ranger could think about was Rufus—where could he be? Had he made it safely inside a classroom? Or was he somewhere else?

Ranger shuddered, remembering how pissed he'd been on Friday night. And if he really let himself think about it, he *could* have interpreted Rufus's reaction as a threat.

After what they saw at Massey's party . . .

"Massey's party . . ." he mumbled. It all made sudden, perfect sense in his mind.

No one responded. They were trying to track the sounds outside, trying to figure out what in the hell was really going on out there.

"It all goes back to that party," Ranger said. "You guys were all there. Theo was there. Hell, even"—he gulped, not wanting to implicate Rufus—"even I was there for a couple of minutes."

No one answered. The silence pressed in on him. "You *know* what I'm talking about," he said flatly. "You all saw what happened."

DRAMA QUEENS

Sage repeated the directions over and over in her head as she sped toward Massey's exclusive neighborhood. It was easy to see where she needed to go. There were dozens of cars lining the street and music pumping from every window of the house.

Sage rushed inside, pushing her way through the throbbing mass of bodies. Paisley's face was burned into her mind's eye as she played a kind of mental match-up game—searching for the identical image in that chaotic crowd. She wanted to scream Paisley's name into the huge room, let her know she was there, but she was afraid it might upset her, embarrass her, make matters for her even worse.

Plus, there was always the possibility that she was totally wrong—that Paisley wasn't even there.

She kept on pushing her way through, unseen. Invisible. The crowd had its own current, like a river, wanted to take her in its own direction instead of where she wanted to be.

No, she thought, allowing instinct to be her guide. She spun around and found a hallway behind her— a long hallway, packed with people. Her brow crumpled. *Down there?* she wondered.

And then she saw a familiar head of tousled brown hair.

Sage propelled herself forward. "Theo?" she called. "Theo!"

He turned, his face registering confusion and a little bit of fear. "Sage, Paisley's down the hall," he said. "With Stone."

"Oh my God," Sage whispered, ramming herself into the crowd. "We have to get her!"

She could see him, Stone, standing head and shoulders above almost everyone else. She bobbed back and forth, peering around heads to see what was happening.

Stone had his hands on Paisley's chest as he tried to kiss her; she was just barely avoiding his mouth as she stretched her arms against his massive body. She managed to push his hands away, but they went immediately down to her skirt, then up underneath it. She pushed against him, screamed, and although he stumbled backward, he recovered quickly. His entire face sank into a frown as he crushed her against the opposite wall with his full weight. His hands went to her hips, yanking her into him. He tried to pull her blouse open, but she shoved him again, this time with a surprising burst of strength.

Stone bounced backward, off the opposite wall.

The manic activity in the hallway seemed to come to a halt for a moment, everyone realizing at the same time what just happened: Paisley Reed had rejected Stone, and now the buttons from her top were bouncing all over the floor.

"Bitch!" he slurred. He grabbed Paisley by the arm, threw his shoulder against one of the bedroom doors—and then they were gone.

Sage gasped. Rushed forward with Theo right behind her. Which room had Stone had gone into? She opened a door to her left, then one to her right. Couples yelled, bodies scrambled to cover themselves, but none of them were Paisley.

And then she heard it—even over the intense volume of music and laughter, there were screams. And they were coming from the last door in the hall.

Sage pounced on the knob, but it was locked. She turned to Theo, frantic.

Theo threw himself against the door, and to Sage's utter shock, it flew open. She scrambled into the room.

Paisley was on the bed, her skirt up around her waist. The little green cami was splayed open, not one button left to protect her modesty. Stone's jeans were around his thighs.

Theo gaped at the scene. "Son of a—"

Sage had no idea where she found the vodka bottle or when she picked it up, but as Stone turned, disoriented, she swung it at him. The force of the blow knocked him to the floor.

Paisley was still crying as Sage clutched at her hand, reeling her in. Theo led them out of the bedroom and down the hall. But no one bothered to come to their assistance. Instead of rushing to her aid, they were laughing at the sight of her partially naked body. Circles of black mascara began to form under her eyes.

As Sage continued to thread her way through the crowd, she spotted Nicole McClintock standing down the hall near Paisley. She watched in horror as Nicole's eyes locked onto Paisley's and then dropped to her exposed chest.

Nicole burst into shrieking laughter at the spectacle, the sound piercing even through the elevated decibels of an out-of-control house party. The others standing in the hallway joined Nicole, their laughter intensifying as Paisley stood there clutching her torn shirt together in vain.

"Paisley!" Sage began to scream. "Paisley—don't let go of me!"

She feared that at any moment they could be separated. That she'd lose Paisley forever, pulled away by a powerful undertow.

Paisley threw herself around Sage and clung to her, terrified, like a child.

"Theo," Sage leaned over and shouted in his ear. "Help me!"

Theo rushed in and scooped Paisley up in his arms. "Hang on to me," he instructed as he tried to push his way through the crowd.

The sharp edge of laughter followed them down the hallway as they fought to squeeze past. Paisley wound her arms tightly around Theo's chest.

When they got out to the sidewalk, Theo stopped and set Paisley gently down. He instinctively pulled the loose sides of her shirt together as he guided her over to Sage.

"Can you get her home by yourself?" he asked.

Sage frowned. "Aren't you coming?"

"I can't," he told her. He turned a steely gaze

toward the house. "There's something I need to go back and finish."

Sage watched, baffled, as he took one slow step and then another before dissolving once again into the crowded party.

PREPS

"OKAY, LIKE, WHAT THE hell was that?" Nicole snipped, finally helping Brittany find Stone after an exhaustive search. "Why would he try to do some drama queen when he could totally have *you*?!"

Brittany took a long sip of beer, her face twisting from the bitterness of it. "I don't know." She shivered. "Maybe this wasn't such a good idea."

"He might be an eentsy bit drunk," Nicole suggested, then rushed to add, "But don't let that confuse things, okay? Look, there he goes! See? He's walking away. He's not the least bit interested in her. Go, Brittany, make your move, now!"

As Nicole watched Brittany edge her way down the hall, that drama queen, Paisley, and her friend, Miss Armpit Hair, passed her going the other direction. Paisley had her boobs hanging out of a cami knockoff that looked like it came off the sales rack at Kmart. She couldn't help herself; the laughter scrambled out of her mouth before she could stop it. It was kind of funny. In a totally lame, pathetic way.

TECHIES

THE HOUSE WAS SO silent it was a little freaky. Maggie was used to being home alone; it wasn't necessarily that. But she was filled with sudden, suffocating regret about telling Theo to go to that party. Part of her selfishly wished she had kept him there with her, but the other part was less tangible—a nameless fear that something awful could happen.

She thought about calling his cell phone until she discovered, a moment later, that he'd left it on her dresser.

She considered going to Massey's herself, finding him and dragging him out of that hellhole. But all she could think about were all those horrible, insipid movies where the leads wind up in some comedy of errors and spend the whole night chasing each other, never managing to catch up.

She went to the window and stared out, sure that she'd see him roll up any second.

Then she sat on her bed, picked up one of the magazines her mother was always conspicuously leaving around the house. She stared at it in sheer desperation.

Some beautiful blond flavor of the day on the cover beckoned with bedroomy eyes and sultry lips and a body barely contained in something that unfathomably passed for fashion.

Maggie pulled her sweatshirt firmly over her hips. She flipped through the pages, stopping at the advice column. She scoffed at the titles of the letters, supposedly written by the teenage girls who read the magazine.

Day to Night Lip Gloss: Dear Girl Next Door, What's the best way to take the same lip gloss from a busy day at school to a Friday night party?

When No Becomes Maybe: Dear Girl Next Door, My boyfriend has been pushing me to have sex, and I've always said "no." But lately I've been thinking, "Well, maybe . . ."

When You and Your Guy Are Barely Hanging On: Dear Girl Next Door, When my

guy and I first hooked up, it was like, "Wow!"
But it cooled off so fast, and now I'm wondering
what he really sees in me.

Maggie groaned, disgusted. She threw the magazine on her bed, went into the bathroom, and rinsed her face with cool water. When she looked up, she was caught off guard by the face staring back at her.

She thought of the girl on the magazine cover—how every hair was in place—the way her skin just glowed. When her gaze returned to her own reflection, she had trouble looking herself in the eye. She stared so long that the room behind her faded slowly to black, leaving nothing but her own appalling image bouncing back at her.

She leaned in closer. Her rounded face, her reddish skin, the same soft hairs on her upper lip that a lot of girls had—only on her, they looked like a full-blown mustache. God, she was hideous!

She pulled the skin around her nose tight against her face—noticed how big her pores looked in the sallow light of the bathroom.

She jerked back. *Oh, yeah,* she thought. *And then there's this.*

In her green sweatshirt and jeans, Maggie couldn't help thinking she looked like a trout, round in the middle, mouth opening and closing in desperation. In insatiable need.

Suddenly, her extensive wardrobe of fleece sweatshirts no longer seemed adequate. She pulled the sweatshirt off and stood, staring at herself in disgust. She turned sideways, studying her white trout body.

Maggie's hatred resurfaced with a vengeance. She went back into her bedroom, picked up a pad of paper and a pencil.

Dear Girl Next Door, I finally found someone who understands me, who's willing to jump off the building with me if that's what it takes, and what do I do? Send him into the trenches, surrounded by temptation. Who would blame him for finding someone else, someone who's beautiful, easy, uncomplicated? Someone better than me? It sure as hell wouldn't be very hard.

The ringing of the phone cut Maggie's self-loathing rant short.

She ran over to the desk, fumbling for a second with the on button.

"Theo?" she breathed.

"Maggie?"

"Mom?"

"Wait a minute . . . who's Theo?" Her mother's voice had that tone, the one that said, *You're in deep crap*, without actually having to say anything. "I told you, no company, Maggie, especially no b—"

"It's nothing like that." Maggie groaned, quickly thinking up a lie. "It's for a project we're supposed to be working on. It's due Monday. We were going to work on it over the phone, but he . . ."

She walked over to the window, looked out. Nothing.

"I guess he's a no-show." She sighed.

"Okay, well. Did you eat dinner?"

"Yeah, but I really need to go—"

"And you put your dishes in the dishwasher?"

"Yes, Mom. *God*, I put the damn dishes away!"

"Magnolia!" her mother yelped.

"I'm sorry, but it's, like, we go through this every time you work graveyard. Have I ever *not* put my dishes away?"

"I don't want anyone coming over, Maggie," her mother said flatly. "No boys, you hear?"

"Yes, Mother. I *hear* you. But I really have to go now. In case he calls."

"All right. Be good, sweetie. I'll see you in the morning."

Maggie pushed the off button. She held the dead phone in her hand for a minute or two before reluctantly returning it to the base.

She dragged down the stairs, past the bathroom, into the kitchen.

There, in the middle of the table, was the pile of dishes from the quasi-dinner she and Theo had eaten.

Maggie squinched her eyes, heaved a sigh, and reluctantly began clearing them away.

God, where is he? she wondered. What could possibly have sidelined him? She was sure this task was as important to him as it was to her. The only thing she could remotely imagine that could come between Theo and their mission was . . .

No. Paisley Reed would never go to a party like that—would she?

Theo had almost succeeded in making her feel bad about writing that *Metro* article. But she'd stuck by her guns, and now she was glad she did.

As far as Maggie was concerned, Paisley Reed could go straight to hell—right along with the rest of them.

TECHIES

THE LAST THING THEO managed to get on tape was Stone dragging Brittany into one of the bathrooms.

He felt his jaw clench. What was going in there? Sex? Drugs? Whatever it was, Theo was going to get evidence. He was going to bury that son of a bitch so deep he'd never get out. After what he'd done to Paisley, he deserved it.

No, once Theo was through with him, no one would remember Harold Stone with admiration or anything approaching fondness. He'd be exposed as the unfeeling monster that he really was.

Theo stalked forward toward the door, which was still slightly ajar. He had his hand on the knob when he heard someone on the back deck.

"Shit! The cops!"

Suddenly it was pandemonium as everyone scrambled to escape from the house.

Theo kept the camera rolling as he made his way down the hallway and back through the congested living room. For one thing, he didn't have time to reach in his pocket and turn it off; for another, he didn't want to risk getting caught so close to the end of filming. Besides, it turned out to be the best part of the show: half-naked couples pouring out of every possible room, pulling up pants, buttoning up blouses, hopping back into underwear. There were even some completely naked people darting out of the pool, desperately searching for wherever they'd left their clothes. Girls were screaming. Guys, drunk and laughing, dashed for their cars.

Theo made it outside and over to the hedges where he'd ditched his bike coming in. Cars were peeling out of the driveway and away from curbs.

Theo pulled his bike out of the bushes and hopped on, but as he cranked his foot on the pedal, he spun out, his tire catching in a muddy rut. He tried to correct and ran into a jagged landscaping rock instead.

He heard a car engine start up. That's when he realized he was lying partway in the driveway. Gauging by the way everyone else was screeching out of there, Theo figured he had about two seconds to live.

"Jesus Christ!" he muttered as he pulled himself and his bike out from under the back tires of a brand-new sports car. The wheels missed him by inches as the car blasted off down the road, a chorus of gravel and debris crunching underneath.

Theo lay panting in the dirt, wiping the residual fear from his brow as he realized how close he'd just come to being roadkill. He propped himself up on his elbows and was trying to catch his breath when the intermittent flash of squad car lights cast a pulsing red glow on the ground. Faint at first, the lights were definitely getting brighter.

"Shit!" He groaned, struggling to stand up.

The ominous red glow was pouring onto the street brighter and brighter by the second. He looked up and could see the police cruisers about two blocks away now. He started to wonder if he'd ever make it back to Maggie's.

"Theo! Yo, Theo!"

Theo turned to find Rufus and Ranger calling to him from a nearby driveway. "This way, man." They gestured with their hands.

Theo hopped on his bike, ignoring the pain, somewhere around his abdomen. He had to get out of there—cruisers were rolling up to the house.

Theo pedaled like crazy behind Dockins and Ng,

jetting down the driveway and through tiny side streets and alleyways in a desperate bid to escape. No one gave chase. A kid on a bike was pretty small potatoes compared to drunk kids in brand-new sports cars, Theo figured.

He rode and rode, faster than he'd ever needed to, as far as he could remember. It wasn't until he hit the 7-Eleven that Theo allowed himself to slow down and then to stop. He straddled his bike and looked down to assess the damage.

FREAKS

WHEN THEY WERE STILL at the 7-Eleven, Rufus had become overwhelmed by curiosity about the whole jock train that had passed in front of them and about Theo, who seemed to be the caboose. Once he'd talked Ranger into it, they'd followed him, and to Rufus's surprise, they ended up in an upscale neighborhood where the houses were almost as big as their whole high school.

It was obvious there was a party going on. What wasn't so obvious was why Theo Martin was there. It wasn't exactly his crowd.

"Are we gonna hang out here all night?" Ranger asked. "Standing in front of some asshole's house watching a bunch of jocks and preps get drunk is hardly my idea of a good time."

"I just wanna see what's going on, dude," Rufus mumbled, squinting in the direction of the party.

And then, a slight commotion at the front door brought their attention back to the house. When he saw who it was, Rufus's eyebrows shot skyward.

There was Theo Martin, coming out of the front door with Sage Wood and Paisley Reed, who he was carrying in his arms like a baby. They stopped at the end of the walkway. Rufus couldn't hear what they were saying, but then Theo turned around and went back inside. Sage put her arm around Paisley's shoulders and began guiding her down the street. The girls didn't acknowledge Rufus or Ranger at first, even though they crossed the street right in front of them.

But Rufus saw the girls. Paisley's girls, to be exact, which for some reason were hanging out of her shirt. He elbowed Ranger.

"Check *that* out." He smiled.

Ranger's face lit up at the sight. "Hel-lo!" He grinned.

Paisley turned then and stared at them. Rufus pitched back a little, shocked at the black rings under her eyes. He wasn't sure what had happened, but something had gone down at that party—something bad happened to Paisley Reed.

He knew it was wrong to think so, but Paisley looked kind of goth like that, her makeup all smeared. It turned him on a little.

"Shit," he whispered to Ranger. "I hope they didn't hear us."

Not much after that, Rufus heard the wail of sirens—saw the black-and-whites coming to bust things up. Theo Martin stumbled out the front door again, nearly got himself creamed by a bunch of jocks fleeing the scene.

"Theo. Yo, Theo!" Rufus called.

* * *

A little while later, thanks to Ranger's encyclopedic knowledge of shortcuts, they stood in front of the 7-Eleven, panting.

"Hey," Rufus said to Theo by way of a greeting.

"You look like hell, dude," Ranger blurted.

It was tactless but true. Theo was covered with dirt and smeared with mud, and his T-shirt was torn straight across the middle like he'd gotten into a fight with a cyborg.

"I think I just went through hell," Theo mumbled, almost like he was talking to himself.

"Yeah, dude," Ranger said. "You look all Mad Max and stuff."

"What happened?" Rufus asked.

"Damn," Theo said, as if he hadn't heard the question. "Sonofabitch!"

"What is it?"

"You wouldn't believe me if I told you," Theo mumbled, fingering the long rip in his T-shirt.

"You mean the party?" Ranger asked.

Theo looked up. He seemed rattled by the question. "Yeah, I went there to do some filming. But, like, don't say anything, okay?"

"Cool with us," Rufus said.

Ranger cut straight to the chase. "Didja get anything good?"

Theo slowly shook his head. "I guess that depends on what you call 'good.'"

Rufus and Ranger flicked their eyes at each other.

A heavy silence set Theo adrift for a few minutes while Rufus and Ranger tried to figure out what was going on. They shrugged at each other over Theo's bowed head.

"That's okay," Rufus finally said, "you don't have to tell us anything. Just show us your tape, dude."

Theo lifted his eyes, staring first at Ranger, then Rufus. "Are you sure you *want* to see it?"

"It's not like we've never been to a friggin' house party," Rufus said. He felt his cheeks color. "I'm sure it was pretty insane over there."

"You don't know the half of it," Theo mumbled. "Check this out . . ."

*　*　*

Rufus and Ranger sat in mute disbelief as they watched the footage of Massey's party.

The violent truth of what really happened slammed dead center into Rufus's gut. He couldn't stand to see anymore. "Shut it off," he whispered.

Although he was staring right at Theo and Ranger, he couldn't see them through his blinding fury. All he saw were the ghosts of childhood past, coming back to haunt him, one hellish image at a time.

He saw Calvert, when they were in second grade, breaking Rufus's pencils every time he got up from his desk. And Ted Hooks, when they were in third grade, stealing their four-square ball in the middle of their game. In middle school the jocks, led now by Stone, beating up Rufus and Ranger for their lunch money . . .

Jesus, the litany of offenses was too long to recall. And until tonight, the last thing on that list was Stone, busting Rufus's long board in half. But now . . .

Now it had reached a whole new level.

He shook his head. "We just stood there and laughed at Paisley tonight after what Stone did to her."

"Dude," Ranger said, "we didn't know—"

"We should have known!" Spit and ire flew out of Rufus's mouth along with his words. "And more to the point—we *do* know now. It's Stone, man. The guy's been a social hazard since he came to this freaking school!"

Rufus stared hard at Theo. "Do you really think he was trying to *rape* her?"

Theo nodded. Rufus could see his jaw working, trying to contain . . . something. "Looked like it."

"Fuckin'-A," Rufus whispered, his entire body shaking with rage. "I am sick of this, man. Sick of it. So—what are *we* going to do to stop that guy?"

Ranger's eyes popped open. He looked from Rufus to Theo to Rufus again. "What do you mean, *stop him*?"

"He's a destructive force," Rufus stated, locking Theo in his gaze. "It's easy for a Neanderthal like Stone to bust a long board in half—that's just the steroids talking. But he has no idea what destruction really is, man."

He moved closer to Theo, narrowed his eyes. "If it came out of nowhere, if he wasn't expecting it . . . he wouldn't know what hit him.

"Like Stone says," Rufus whispered, "*payback is a bitch.*"

TECHIES

By the time Theo got back to Maggie's, it was way late.

As he pedaled toward her house, in an effort to calm himself, he began to calculate the length of their relationship in a variety of mathematical terms. *If one day were the equivalent of a year, how many years would we have actually been together? Or I could factor in the intensity of each minute we've spent together versus the relative superficiality of most other relationships and calculate the actual value of the time . . .*

Before he got to the point where he needed to use SAT terms to figure the whole thing out, Theo could see Maggie's house just up the street.

A single chunk of throbbing blue light lit the far

back corner of the house, like part of the moon had fractured and fallen into Maggie's room. Theo had a hard time keeping his bike steady as he pulled up the driveway. He was still shaking, he guessed from the unnerving experience of almost losing his life to a wild pack of juiced-up, drunken jocks.

His skin prickled as he dropped the kickstand, and suddenly Theo could feel himself splitting into two distinct beings. There was the old Theo, the guy who had left Maggie's house earlier that night to go to a party and do a little clandestine filming. That Theo couldn't wait to go inside and show Maggie the footage from Massey's place.

But then there was the Theo who had watched Stone attack Paisley at that same party—the Theo who had finally come to see how the Stones and Nicoles of the world would always find a way to screw over people like him.

That Theo couldn't get the hairs on the back of his neck to lie flat because this thing was so huge. And payback, as Rufus had said, needed to be swift and sure.

Payback was what he wanted, after all. What he and Maggie both wanted. So why couldn't he shake his apprehension?

It took nearly five minutes and a number of attempts, knocking louder and louder each time, before she finally answered the door.

"Maggie," he breathed. "God, am I happy to see you!" He swung in for a kiss and she diverted, offering him not quite her cheek—more like a corner of her hair. "Maggie?"

"You're late," she said flatly.

His brows clasped together as he searched her face for empathy. "Did I—did I wake you up?"

"How am I supposed to sleep, with you out there who the hell knows where?" she snapped at him.

"You knew where I was. I was at Massey's party. You sent me there."

Maggie's eyes flashed at him. "I didn't *send* you there! You went because that was the plan."

Theo shook his head. "What are you . . . ?"

"What took you so long to get back?" she demanded, all hellfire and damnation.

His face must have registered his disbelief, but Maggie didn't acknowledge it.

"Look at me," he said, indicating his ripped T-shirt, his filthy jeans. "As you can clearly see, I've had a bit of an ordeal."

She turned and went upstairs without saying another word. Theo followed. In her bedroom the TV was on—some lame infomercial hawking a life-changing acne product.

Maggie whirled on him. "So who was there?"

Theo didn't know why, but he could feel his skin

prickle. "Everyone. I mean . . . it was a friggin' party—"

"No! It was a *simple job*, Theo. Go there, film, come back."

"Jesus Christ, Maggie. What's going on here?"

Maggie picked up the remote control on her nightstand and the TV went suddenly, sharply black.

Neither of them spoke. Theo didn't know what the hell to say.

"Are you going to show me the tape?" Maggie asked at last. The words crackled in the dark like fireworks, spitting and hissing just before they disappeared behind a puff of sulfur.

Ignoring the twisting in his gut, Theo docked his camera to Maggie's computer and turned it on. They sat on the edge of the bed and watched as Theo arrived at the party, tried to negotiate first the entryway, then the living room, which was crammed with kids. Maggie's lips curled in disgust as Nicole and Brittany walked into the party like they owned the place.

Only then did Theo realize what he'd done.

He could feel it coming. He should have *seen* it coming long before now, but he didn't, and now he could feel it, a semi, barreling down on him.

Maggie turned slowly toward him. "Why did you follow Paisley Reed around all night?" she demanded.

Theo couldn't believe his ears. Was Maggie jealous? Of *Paisley Reed*?

"Jesus Christ, Maggie, I did what you asked me to do. I went, I taped, and I came back. What fucked-up sitcom took place here in the relatively small window of time that I was gone??"

"You betrayed me," Maggie whispered.

He was so stunned, it took him several seconds to catch his breath enough to respond. "How did I betray you?"

"We had a deal, Theo. You finish your tape so we could set up our Web site and show all those assholes who really holds the power around here. And instead you come back with a lame episode of the *Paisley Reed Show*. How am I supposed to write a scathing editorial in the *Metro* about the fall of the Elite Empire when all that's on the tape is your pathetic ex-girlfriend?"

Maggie drew in a deep shuddering breath before adding, "You deceived me."

Theo stood up. "You're crazy." He choked back his tears.

He didn't know the layout of her room well enough to feel his way out in pitch black. The sounds of him knocking into her bedpost echoed in the dark. "Shit!"

"Where are you going?" she asked. Theo thought he heard a catch in her voice. Yeah, well. Too late for that now.

"Where am I going? I'm going home! Jesus, Maggie, I thought you were different. But you're not. You're just like them—exactly like them. So yeah, I'm leaving. And the only thing I can even *think* to say to you right now is . . . *see you in the quad sometime.*"

QUAD

In that instant, the police radios faded, and there was nothing but stillness.

Complete, dead calm.

Even the breathing inside the student store seemed to have stopped, as if they'd all just heard someone's heart beat for the last time. People strained for any sound that might help them figure out what was going on outside. The absence of gunshots was nearly as loud as the shots themselves.

Ranger looked around the room, trying to figure out what to make it all mean. Was it almost over? Did the cops have the place surrounded? Or did they only just do that in the movies?

I gotta stop watching so much TV, he couldn't help thinking. But this was real life, and Ranger knew what the deal was.

"God, don't you guys get it?" Ranger continued. "All that shit, man. All that shit we dished out. All of us. This is what it adds up to." Ranger looked around the room, trying to get them all to see what he now saw so clearly. "And then? After Massey's party? It just got to be too much. Do you get it? Too fucking much!"

For a moment, there was nothing but the sound of breathing inside the store. Ranger turned his head and noticed Sage Wood, watching him intently. He set his gaze on her and didn't let go. "After a while . . ." he said to her, keeping his voice as low as he could. "After a while, a person can just—snap."

Sage's head tilted to one side, heavy with confusion.

"It was just too much," he repeated softly.

Her eyes grew wide. Fearful. She began to shake her head. "No," she said. "You're wrong."

A burst of movement and noise just outside the building put everyone inside on alert.

"Drop the weapon!" they heard someone shout with authority. The sound of voices fading in and out over two-way radios drifted into the store through the windows. They heard a flurry of footsteps too, muffled by the grass and dirt surrounding the small building.

"I said, drop it, Miss!"

Maggie's head snapped in the direction of the door. *"Miss?"* she yelped.

"Slowly!"

"Oh my God!" Sage cried out in a panic. "No, it can't be."

She jumped to her feet, rushing to the door. "Move the chest," she called over to Calvert and Stone. *"Move it!"*

No one scrambled to accommodate her. They just sat, dumbstruck, as she heaved herself against the freezer. "No!" she screamed as her tiny body struck the large metal box. "No! Don't hurt her!"

One last shove allowed just enough of an opening for Sage to squeeze herself out the door.

Ranger slid over and peered through the narrow opening.

There was Paisley Reed, sitting on the ground just outside the student store. She was crumpled to her knees in the dirt, a small revolver lying in her lap.

She looked strangely pretty, Ranger thought, her vintage dress billowing softly around her, sunlight catching in her hair. But the blood . . . Jesus, she was spattered with blood . . .

Sage tried to run to Paisley, but a huge officer in a Kevlar vest grabbed her with one arm, pulled her toward his chest.

Sage kicked and screamed. "Please!" she begged one of the officers whose gun was still trained on Paisley. "Don't hurt her! It's not her fault!"

The small revolver in Paisley's lap fell to the ground as she finally seemed to notice someone she recognized. "Sage?"

Ranger saw Paisley's lips speak the single word. But she looked confused, like she'd just woken from a dream.

Sage shrieked, squirmed out of the officer's grip, and ran onto the quad. She dove toward Paisley, gathered the heap of her into her arms.

The officer following Sage reached down and swiftly confiscated the revolver. "Suspect disarmed," he said into his radio. "We're clear!"

Sage wrapped her arms around Paisley, stroked her hair, wiped the tears from her cheeks. One by one, the others inched out of the student store, gathering in stunned silence as Sage Wood sat in the grass, rocking Paisley Reed like a child.

Paisley shuddered, her gaze drifting across the quad. "They were so mean to me." Her dark eyes rose to meet Sage's. "Why do people have to be so mean?"

Ranger was the last to come out of the store, exiting just as Nicole McClintock rushed to the scene. She looked like hell, Ranger thought ruefully. Tears had washed all the makeup off her face, and there were bloodstains all over her expensive clothes.

"You killed her!" she shouted as the officers tried to calm her. "Oh my God, you killed her!"

As the police gently eased Nicole away, Ranger's eyes found Hayley Banks, cowering behind a concrete planter box. She too had Brittany's blood on her.

Ken Davis spotted her then, rushed to her side, and folded her into his arms. Hayley crumpled against him as she burst into tears.

Calvert grabbed Stone's arm to get his attention, nodding in their direction. Stone stood and watched in disbelief as Ken embraced Hayley. He shook off Calvert's grip, then turned away.

Ranger scanned the crowd of faces that were slowly moving into the quad from the surrounding doorways and classrooms. For a moment he panicked, and then he spotted Rufus coming out of the cafeteria.

He gave Rufus a silent nod.

Rufus held Ranger's gaze for a moment, then shook his head. The triceratops horns on the top of his head barely moved. He spun around, walking away from the center of the quad even as teachers and students were rushing in to see what was going on there. Ranger cast one last glance at the crowd gathered in front of the student store, then turned to follow Rufus.

Over his shoulder, Ranger could still hear Paisley crying. Her words grew fainter the farther he walked, but he could still hear them. Still hear her as she cried.

"Why? Why do people have to be so mean?"

ACKNOWLEDGMENTS

BECAUSE THIS IS MY first book, my inclination is to thank everyone in the known universe—from my mail carrier to the girl who sold me coffee the day I got "the call" from Razorbill. And I know I can't do that. But the truth is, it takes a village to write a book. Just ask the following people —they belong to mine, and I thank them with bottomless gratitude:

My agent, Laura Rennert (unimaginably patient and supportive); my editor, Kristen Pettit (brilliant, yet always amusing); my husband and children (three of the coolest people on the planet, and I'm not just saying that); Karen and Feven (for being real with me) and the rest of my critique posse—including Tom, Jan, Julie, Doug, Naheed, Pennie, Liahna, Liz, Jennifer, Ilene, Sylvie, and the ladies from the

SCBWI retreat; my friends at Challenge Day (inspirational to the tenth power); and the rest of my family for riding this roller-coaster ride along with me . . .

And for all the kids who have the courage to face their own quad every day . . .